WARRIOR DEMONESS

Book VI
The Illusionist Series

by

Fran Heckrotte

2016

Warrior Demoness

Sixth in The Illusionist series

Copyright © 2008 by Fran Heckrotte
Smashwords Edition
All rights reserved.

eBook ISBN: 978-1-939950-17-8
Print ISBN: 978-1-939950-19-2

First Edition eBook Format: June 2009

This book is Published by
Novel Ideas Publishing, LLC
Beaufort, SC. USA

Cover Design by Patty Henderson
Email: pattyghenderson@aol.com

Copy Editor: Cindy Burke
Email: cindyburkeoriginals@gmail.com

Acknowledgments

A special thanks to my beta readers who helped me with the stories of Saira and Warrior Demoness. They have traveled with me on my journey in creating the Illusionist series and were instrumental in getting me to my destination. Alex D'Brassis, Lee McLean, and Kimberly, my betas...and Mary K. Bosshart, my alpha reader.

To Pam, your help is invaluable in both beta reading and proofing my stories. Thanks so much for all your hard work.

Patty G. Henderson, my cover artist. Everyone who sees your creations is amazed at your ability to capture the essence of each story. The covers are phenomenal.

To A.L., thanks for encouraging me to write.

And yes, to Howie, who is still wondering why I mention him.

Citizens and Denizens of the Underworld by Hierarchy
The Illusionist Series

Dis - The Underlord of the Underworld

All who serve at Dis' pleasure belong to castes, although it isn't viewed that way by the inhabitants.

Demons and Demonesses - No specific designations. Normally are left to their own devices unless called upon by Dis. Ambitious, most seek power and influence. Some want to overthrow Dis while others are satisfied serving him.

Minions - Servants and warriors. Capable of achieving high positions in the Underworld.

Hordlings - Foot soldiers. Low intelligence, highly trainable and dependable.

Imps - Mischief makers and messengers. Rarely dependable except when Dis is involved.

Citizens of the Overworld
*Belong to an established caste system
but can rise to other levels.*

The Twin - Master of the Overworld, Tinkerer.

Seraphim - Upper Management.

Throne - All-seeing entities.

Powers - Exalted servants and warriors.

Virtues - Servants and warriors.

Dominions - Servants, gentle natured.

Principalities - Messengers and warriors.

Archangels - Enforcers of the rules and laws.

Angels - General term for all the inhabitants of the Overworld.

THE GREAT BATTLE
Prequel

CHAPTER 1

DARK CRIMSON AND bright orange rivers flowed across the Neutral Zone like a plague...only worse. The unnatural brew created a deadly combination of toxic gases, turning the Zone into a vast wasteland void of all life — with the exception of those of the Overworld and Underworld.

Demon and Angel blood were never meant to be mixed. The two races could interact with each other for short periods, but coexistence was impossible. Demons required the heat from the Hellfires to replenish their energies, while Angels needed the cool, crisp environment of the Overworld to nourish theirs.

For this reason alone, the Great Battle could only take place in the shadowy realm that separated Heaven and Hell, and many from both worlds questioned their masters' judgment for continuing a war that had ceased to have meaning. Few, however, dared to voice such doubts.

* * *

The warriors were exhausted. Both sides refused to give an inch...and so the Army of the Overworld and the Legions of the Underworld struggled on. Only their masters could stop the bloodshed, and few believed that it would happen. Neither Dis nor his Twin was willing to concede to the other, and so the battle continued as it had for tens of thousands of years.

Many brethren and sisters had succumbed to the continued onslaught of a campaign that no longer served a purpose. The survivors grew weary of carrying their destroyed comrades home...at least those that could be found. There were some who simply vanished, leaving no bodies to mourn. That emptiness left the living unsettled. Life deserved the finality of death and the honors that went with it. Immortality was no longer a reality once the Great Battle had begun.

* * *

Dis stood on his balcony, staring into the distant eternal fires of the Underworld. They danced and swayed almost magically as their orange and red flames leapt upward, seeking to embrace the iridescent blue sky. Aware that he was being watched by the remaining commanders of his Legions, Dis chose to ignore them awhile longer. As Underlord, he knew the value of patience – their patience.

The last hundred battles hadn't gone well. Many of his Legions had been destroyed and several of his dead had vanished.

Vanished, he thought. *The best of my best and even I don't know where they have gone. Death pretends to know nothing. I find that hard to believe.* Shaking his head, he turned to look at the small group who waited for him to speak. Mentally taking an inventory of the twenty-three demons, he felt a momentary remorse at the loss of those who were missing.

"Alocer," he called out, motioning for the lion-faced demon to step forward.

"My Lord," Alocer replied, respectfully bowing his head. His golden mane fell forward, concealing the bright, reddish-brown eyes.

"It's good to see you," Dis said, grasping the demon's shoulders with his massive hands. "How is Plorax? Has she fared well in the battles?"

Alocer raised his head and smiled. Dis forgot nothing, including the name of Alocer's white horse. As a demon knight, Alocer was proud of Plorax. The mare was brave, intelligent, and fearless.

"She is well, My Lord, and anxious for our next battle."

Dis laughed. "Good! And your Legions?"

Again Alocer bowed his head...this time in shame. "Of the thirty-three, only seventeen remain."

"Seventeen is better than nothing, Alocer. Return to them. Tell them of my gratitude for their sacrifices and loyalty. As a reward, I am granting them a few days off to celebrate their victories."

"But the Battle, My Lord. They are needed–"

"A few days won't affect something that has been going on for so long. The rest will invigorate them. Now go!"

Bowing at the waist, Alocer turned and walked away. It wasn't for him to question his master.

"Berith." Dis called the next commander forward. A large, red demon with two horns protruding from his forehead snapped to attention and then stepped in front of the Underlord. No one could mistake the family resemblance. Only the descendants of Dis grew the distinct horns of their sire.

"Father," he replied, not making eye contact with Dis.

"You look well, Berith."

"I am."

"How many Legions do you now govern?" Dis asked.

"Almost twenty-one. I trained them well," Berith proclaimed proudly.

"I would expect nothing less from my offspring," Dis chastised. Berith was ambitious. Dis had no doubt his son would one day challenge him for the position of Underlord. It would be disappointing if Berith didn't. Like those before him, though, Berith would fail. There could only be one ruler of the Underworld and it would always be Dis. Still, ambition made Berith a good leader and Dis appreciated good leaders. "Go! Ready your Legions for the next battle."

"As you command, Father." Berith turned and marched out, his head held high. As one of the oldest of Dis' children, royal blood ran hot through his veins, making him both arrogant and competent. It was a deadly combination.

One by one, Dis called his commanders forward to ask about the Legions and to mentally calculate how many remained. When all had left but the last, he motioned for her to sit. Tall and graceful, she strode to a nearby chair and lowered herself onto the seat. As always, Dis was impressed by the demoness' confident demeanor and beauty. Had she not been one of his best Legionnaires, he would have seduced her a long time ago. Dis never questioned his sexual prowess. No one would refuse the advances of the Underlord.

Except Lilith, he thought and mentally chuckled. Noticing the black orchid tattoo below the commander's left eye, he was reminded of Orchidrina.

"Do you still mourn her, Sabnock?" he asked.

"No, My Lord. I only regret we have never found her body. She deserved better."

"As do all who have never come back. You have honored her well, though. No other Legionnaire has earned thirteen Flames," Dis said, referring to the tattoos on her arms and legs. Each one represented the destruction of twenty-three Battalions of the Twin's Army.

Sabnock had personally led the attacks. Few of Dis' senior officers liked to command from the front lines, and with good reason. Archangels were tenacious fighters, willing to sacrifice everything for the Twin. "Perhaps one day we'll discover what happened to those who have vanished."

"Perhaps, My Lord."

Dis' eyes narrowed slightly. Sabnock was never one to waste words. It was a trait he both admired and appreciated, though he sometimes wished he knew what she was thinking.

Why is it only the females I find so unfathomable? Dismissing the thought, he decided not to waste any more time.

"The battle isn't going well," he stated calmly.

"No, My Lord. We have lost sixty-three Legions. Nineteen alone belonged to Ronwe."

"Ronwe was an idiot. I never should have put him in charge of so many Legions."

"True," Sabnock agreed.

Unused to criticism, Dis glared at the demoness, his reddish-brown eyes burning brightly as orange flames danced in their depths. When she refused to cower under his gaze, he gave her a faint nod of respect. Sabnock was an anomaly amongst his commanders. She wasn't ambitious, and she spoke the truth, no matter what the consequences. Others would often tell Dis what they thought he wanted to hear.

"You have never feared me, have you, Sabnock?"

The demoness' stoic expression was expected, although Dis was sure she was surprised by his question.

"Why would I fear you, My Lord? You're a hard taskmaster, but fair to those who serve you well."

Dis' eyes gleamed with a suppressed humor.

"Then I must be getting soft," he mused aloud. "Tell me, what do my subjects say about the war?"

"I don't understand the question," Sabnock replied.

"Come, Commander. You know exactly what I mean. What do my people have to say about the war? Many of their comrades have been destroyed. Others have disappeared. Do they blame me or Lilith for this?"

"Your subjects are loyal to you. It's not their place to blame or question their master."

"Said like a good soldier. But, that isn't what I want to hear. Come, Sabnock, you have never been shy about the truth."

Sabnock shook her head. "There are grumblings, but they mean nothing. Merely venting. As your mate, Lilith is highly respected and feared."

"And if she wasn't my mate?"

"She would still be respected and feared. Lilith has adapted well to the Underworld. She takes an interest in everyone and everything here. Her curiosity is insatiable. Her powers are intimidating. Because of you, she has access to areas that normally would be difficult for an outsider to enter. Lilith knows how to take advantage of her resources."

Dis wasn't surprised. Since he had spirited her away from the Twin and transformed her from human to demoness, Lilith's first passion was knowledge.

There once was a time when it was passion, he thought. Her lust had always been insatiable, making her the perfect mate for the Underlord. For that reason alone, he wouldn't have tolerated anyone disrespecting her.

"Is there anything else you wish to know, My Lord?" Sabnock asked, interrupting Dis' thoughts.

Leaning back in his chair, Dis crossed his right leg over his left and glanced down at his foot, a shiny, red hoof.

"Your thoughts," he replied, and hesitated a moment before continuing. "You're an excellent commander and strategist. You have lost only two Legions in over seven thousand years. No one else has been as successful as you in winning battles. I can think of no other more deserving of my respect and gratitude."

"I serve, My Lord," Sabnock said.

For Dis, the answer epitomized everything he knew about the demoness. She was loyal, dedicated and performed her duties without question or doubt. The "without question" part was her greatest attribute because it had nothing to do with Dis or his expectations.

Sabnock understood exactly what he wanted from her. She had never asked for his permission, nor sought his council. It wasn't necessary. Her skills were legendary and feared by enemy and ally alike. It was too bad there was only one Sabnock. The Great Battle would have ended eons ago.

"Well said," he responded. "And because you do, I now seek your thoughts on a matter."

Sabnock's eyes widened slightly. Dis knew he had surprised her and was pleased. It always felt good to shake her normally controlled persona.

"Lilith believes it's time to end this war. She has asked that I offer a truce. What do you think about this?" *Demanded is more like it,* he thought, remembering her threat if he didn't.

"It's not my place to question my Mistress," Sabnock said.

"I'm not asking that you question her...only your thoughts. As one of my most respected commanders, do you think it serves a purpose to carry this war any further?"

"Many have been destroyed on both sides, My Liege. The cause was just, but..." Sabnock hesitated.

"But..."

Sabnock straightened in her chair as if preparing for battle.

"But was it worth the loss? If you're asking for my honest opinion, then it should have ended a long time ago...that is, *if* you and the Twin could ever agree on the terms of a truce. Even now it may be impossible."

"Nothing is impossible. My twin is arrogant, stubborn, and unreasonable. Nonetheless, he values his servants. They are important to the welfare of the Overworld. Their ranks are diminishing as quickly as mine."

"Perhaps more quickly," Sabnock added. "Soon your twin may have to call upon his hierarchy to continue the war."

"It would almost be worth continuing the fight to see the Seraphim getting their chaste, unsullied hands bloodied," Dis said. The thought of his twin's highest caste fighting was laughable. "Is there anyone you can contact on the other side that can carry a message to the Overlord?"

"Possibly. I believe Chameil would be willing to carry a message. She is the most reasonable of the Seraphim and has a special relationship with him."

"I've heard of her. Her honor is almost as legendary as your battle skills. Few have dared to challenge my brother and yet I hear she refused to order his followers into battle. It's rumored that she supported Lilith's decision to leave Paradise."

"So it is said. Chameil would be too respectful to challenge her master publicly, and too honorable to go against her beliefs. I have no doubt there is truth in the stories," Sabnock said.

"Good. She's just the one I need to present my offer. I'll prepare it. Return tomorrow..." He paused. "Sabnock. This must remain between you and me. It will be taken as a sign of weakness if rumors reach the ears of some."

"I understand, My Lord. I will be discreet."

Nodding, Dis stood.

"Walk with me and I'll tell you my plan. Even in my own home there are ears that hear too much."

Rising, Sabnock followed Dis down a corridor and into an enormous garden filled with plants, statues and brilliantly colored fire-fountains. Waves of flames flowed down white marbled tiers, their journey ending in pools of swirling, glowing lava. Known as the Garden of Fire, it was one of the few places the Underlord knew to be free of prying eyes and ears.

Motioning for Sabnock to be seated near a smaller fountain, he told her what he wanted. Minutes later the demoness stood, bowed her head respectfully, and left. Dis watched her disappear through a gate on the far side of the garden and then he returned to his quarters in search of Lilith. She would be pleased — and a pleased Lilith was an exciting Lilith.

CHAPTER 2

LAMASHTU PACED BACK and forth, agitated that Sabnock had not yet returned from the Underlord's castle. Obsessively jealous, she couldn't help but imagine Dis, in his magnificence, seducing her lover. His sexual prowess and appetites were well-known and his skills legendary.

Picking up a small, crystalline statue, she flung it angrily against the far wall and cursed when it didn't shatter as expected.

"I'll kill her," she muttered as the air crackled from her uncontrolled temper.

"You'll kill who?" a voice behind her asked.

Spinning around, Lamashtu saw Sabnock standing in the archway of the room.

"You," Lamashtu replied. "I'll kill you if you let that...that *demon* bed you."

Sabnock laughed. "You mean Dis? Don't be ridiculous. I have no interest in him in that way. Besides, it's not up to you to tell me who I share my favors with."

Unbuckling her sword, she tossed it on the table and then strode purposefully toward her angry lover. "I've warned you before, Lamashtu. Keep up these jealous rages and I'll send you back to the front line. You serve at my pleasure. I decide who, when, and how. Never forget that. Now, pick that up."

"I will not!" Lamashtu replied. Haughtily tossing her head, she turned her back on the demoness.

Grabbing her shoulder, Sabnock turned Lamashtu around and pulled the arrogant demoness close. She held Lamashtu's head in an iron grip and captured her lips forcefully, separating them with her tongue. Lamashtu whimpered with excitement. She loved being dominated. Pulling back, Sabnock's eyes blazed with passion and anger.

"Never challenge me, Lamashtu. You're here to serve my needs and nothing more."

"Then let me serve you now," Lamashtu begged. Sabnock stepped back and smiled. Without comment she strolled into the bedroom. Lamashtu was a skilled lover. A few hours being attended to by her would be pleasant enough.

* * *

Eyes closed, Sabnock allowed Lamashtu free access to her body. The sensation of the hot tongue running leisurely up and down her thigh was both stimulating and relaxing. Small flames trailed the moist lips as they caressed her sensitive skin. Blood as hot as molten iron surged through her veins, sending her body temperature soaring, and still Sabnock controlled her arousal.

Her reputation for being difficult to please was well-earned. Few had the skills or the endurance to bring her to the brink of an orgasm, let alone push her over the edge. Those that could, though, were richly rewarded, and if extremely accomplished, were allowed to share Sabnock's quarters. Lamashtu had lived there for almost three-hundred years. Only one other had managed to stay longer.

Tragically, Orchidrina had been destroyed by the Archangel Uriana in one of the fiercest battles of the war. Although Sabnock had never loved anyone, she was fondest of Orchidrina and missed her greatly. Archangel Uriana's Battalions had suffered dearly for Sabnock's loss. Thousands of Powers and other Angels were destroyed by the demoness' fiery sword.

Uriana would have been too, had Archangels Jorielle, Michael, and ten other warriors not come to her rescue. Even Sabnock's prowess was no match against such powerful foes. She was forced to retreat, leaving her lover's body behind.

I should have brought you back. That mist! It was moving so fast...and I hesitated. It was *that* thought that continually haunted Sabnock. *You deserved a proper cremation.*

Distracted by the memory, Sabnock pushed Lamashtu aside and climbed out of bed. Wiping her mouth with her hand, Lamashtu gave her a curious look.

"Did you not find my attentions pleasing?"

"Pleasing enough," Sabnock replied, grabbing her breeches and slipping them on.

"Pleasing enough? That's not very flattering."

"When have I ever flattered you, Lamashtu? You're an accomplished lover. Not necessarily the best, but better than most. Otherwise you wouldn't be here."

Sabnock ducked as a ball of fire whizzed past her head. Although it wouldn't have hurt her, she strode purposefully to Lamashtu, grabbed her throat in her right hand and squeezed hard.

"I have warned you before about these tantrums. I do not tolerate disrespect from anyone — especially you. You serve at my pleasure. Apparently you haven't learned that yet. Now, get out before I lose my temper."

Pushing the stunned demoness away, Sabnock turned and walked from the room without looking back. The fear in Lamashtu's eyes was piercing. The warrior demoness would not return.

CHAPTER 3

CHAMEIL STARED AT the billowy clouds swirling in the crystalline orb on the table.

"Where are you, Lymineah?" she asked.

The Dominion had been gone too long. She should have returned to her duties four cycles back. Unfortunately, even the powerful Seraphim Chameil couldn't see what lay hidden in the clouds covering the battlefield. Because of her Master's alchemy and that of the Underlord, it was now nearly impossible to penetrate the swirling mass of gases concealing the Neutral Zone which lay between the Overworld and the Underworld. Neutral was perhaps a misnomer, but it was the one area that neither group held an advantage...nor would the immense powers of heaven or hell be very effective. Physical strength and numbers determined the victor.

Shortly after the Great Battle began, Dis had created an impenetrable curtain of fog to hide his minions and demons during an attempt to invade the camps of the Twin's Army. To protect his own servants, the Twin countered with his own concoction of mists.

The result was disastrous. All mortal life in the area was destroyed. Neither demon nor Angel could see beyond a few footsteps, with two exceptions — the Thrones, who were multi-eyed servants of the Twin, and a small number of demons with a unique homing sense. No matter where they went, they always knew how to return to to their respective worlds.

The Thrones were like spinning wheels, stirring up the clouds and sending them into the distance. Large, iridescent eyes gave them the ability to peer into the dense fog and see shapes. They would have given the Twin's Army a tremendous advantage were it not for two problems. Their inability to do anything but spin made them easy targets, and there were fewer Thrones than any other of the Twin's hierarchy. Only one could be spared to guide each Army unit through the ever-changing mists.

Not all of the Neutral Zone was hidden, though. Small clearings appeared and disappeared, constantly shifting amongst the clouds. They provided temporary battlefields for the warring factions. Each army maneuvered in and out of these areas, cautiously aware that they were vulnerable to attack from the enemy concealed in the adjoining mists.

Ferocious battles ensued, resulting in massive injuries and losses on both sides. Unfortunately, because these places were in constant flux, it was sometimes impossible for all of the mortally wounded to be removed before the fog swept in.

Summoning one of her most trusted Thrones, Chameil watched with interest as the spinning entity sailed into her chamber, its many eyes surveying everything around it.

"You wish to see me, Mistress?" it asked, coming to a complete stop in order to focus three of its eleven eyes on Chameil.

"Yes, Thryn. Lymineah is still missing. She's nowhere to be found. Take as many Thrones as can be spared and search for her. She's always been curious about the Zone, so she may have gone there. Her curiosity is always getting her into trouble. This time it may have cost her her life."

"As you command, Mistress." Whirling at a high speed, Thryn disappeared.

* * *

Lymineah knew she had made a mistake.

"A mistake. That's putting it mildly," she murmured.

The Zone wasn't what she had imagined. Hiding in the open wasn't the most comforting decision, but her chances of being found by an Angel were better than if she moved into the mist. She had already been away from her mistress longer than planned. Chameil would be worried, with good reason. The Neutral Zone was unforgiving to those foolish or negligent enough to enter without a Throne.

Mistress Chameil always said my curiosity would be my downfall.

Glancing around, Lymineah shivered. Dismal gray clouds danced eerily in the distance. Occasionally, ominous misty tentacles snaked toward her, twisting and turning as if searching for something to grasp or embrace. Lymineah had the eerie feeling they were after her.

It's just my overactive imagination, she thought, but couldn't shake off a sense of foreboding. Thousands of Angels and demons had been lost to the mysteries hidden amid the whirling masses.

A movement to her left startled Lymineah. Huddling into a tight ball, she tried to make herself as small as possible, knowing it was a ridiculous attempt at hiding. The barren area surrounding her was devoid of everything except the Dominion. Closing her eyes, she prayed that one of her Master's Thrones or Powers would emerge from the clouds. Even a Principality or Virtue would be better than being alone, although they were the lesser of the hierarchies, and not the best fighters.

"At least they'd be company," she muttered.

"What have we here?" a deep, silky voice asked. Lymineah opened one eye barely wide enough to peep through, stared at the warrior standing in front of her...and swallowed. Fear made her arms and legs tingle and then go numb. A large sword hung by the woman's side. Several flame tattoos covered bare arms and legs. "Can you not speak, Dominion? Your kind is notorious for their chattering tongues."

Lymineah knew she needed to say something...anything. To her embarrassment, a raspy squeak was all that slipped past her dry lips.

The warrior pulled her sword from its scabbard.

I'm dead!

Lymineah's eyes rolled back in her head and she toppled over, paralyzed by the thought of never seeing her homeland again.

"I guess the other stories are true, too. You definitely don't tolerate stress well," the warrior said.

CHAPTER 4

SABNOCK SHOOK HER head in disgust as she secured her sword and knelt beside the terrified Dominion. Normally timid creatures, the demoness was surprised to find one alone in the zone.

"You have nothing to fear from me," she said. "My honor would be severely compromised if I destroyed the defenseless, let alone a Dominion." When the Dominion didn't move, Sabnock grasped her under her small wings and lifted her to her feet.

"Come on. Snap out of it. Contrary to what you've heard, demons don't eat Dominions — only imps and an occasional hordling do that. Besides, I'm not going to carry you all the way back to the Gate, so stand up."

Feeling the Dominion relax, Sabnock made sure she was steady on her feet before taking a step back. "Good. We need to talk. You *can* talk, can't you?"

The Dominion nodded reluctantly.

"What do you call yourself?" Sabnock demanded, and sighed when she received no answer. "Listen. My Legions will arrive soon. If they find you here, you will be destroyed and I won't stop them. They have lost a lot of friends and family. Either you answer me now or I'll leave you to them...and one of the imps just might decide to cook you for dinner. Now, what's your name?"

"Ly...Lymin...eah."

"Lylymineah?"

"No, Lymin...eah."

"Well, Lymin...eah, what are you doing in the Zone? You obviously don't belong to the Twin's Army."

"I...I was curious."

"Curious? About what?"

"About the Zone. I've heard so much about it. It's mysterious and foreboding and...and wonderful in an awful way."

Sabnock's forehead crinkled as she listened to the Dominion's ridiculous explanation.

You are either very naïve or mentally defective, she thought.

"This place is neither mysterious nor wonderful. It's an unnatural wasteland that's deadly to all who enter, one way or another. You were foolish to come here. Where's your Throne?"

"I didn't bring one. Chameil would never have approved such a request."

"I would hope not. Is Chameil your Mistress?"

"Yes, and she's very powerful. If you harm me..."

"If I wanted to harm you, you would be harmed by now. You're fortunate that I'm the one who discovered you here. You would provide a great deal of entertainment for some of my warriors...and food for others. Imps and hordlings love sampling your kind. Now, come with me. I have a message for Chameil."

Grasping the Dominion's arm, Sabnock strolled purposefully into the clouds. She could sense several of her scouts approaching and didn't want to be seen talking with one of the Twin's followers. It would provide fodder for those who coveted her job as commander, and Dis had made his position clear about her mission. She was on her own. The Underlord had an image to maintain. If the Great Battle was to end, it had to be the Twin that initiated a truce...or at least be perceived that way.

* * *

"Where have you been?" Chameil demanded, her eyes blazing angrily at Lymineah. "And don't tell me it was the Neutral Zone."

Lymineah bowed her head and said nothing. Chameil leaned forward, tipping her own head sideways to peer more closely at the small Dominion.

"Why don't you answer me? Are you ill?"

"No," Lymineah whispered.

"Then tell me where you've been."

"I can't."

"Why not?"

"You told me not to."

Chameil frowned and straightened up.

"I did no such thing," she replied, then realized her mistake. "Oh. You *were* in the Zone."

Lymineah nodded.

"You disobeyed me. Of all my Dominions, you have always been the most trustworthy."

"I'm sorry, Mistress."

"Why would you take such a risk? What is it about the Zone that is so important you have forsaken your vow of obedience?"

Lymineah raised her head and looked into Chameil's eyes.

"I was curious. There are so many stories..."

"You were willing to sacrifice everything because of stories? I'm disappointed in you. I have already petitioned for your advancement to Virtue. Now, there is no way you will be accepted into the next hierarchy. Was it worth it, Lymineah?" Chameil asked. She was saddened that her servant had given up everything for something as insignificant as curiosity.

"I met a demon!" Lymineah suddenly blurted out, unable to contain her excitement. "She was magnificent...tall and powerful...and—"

"You met a demon? How is that possible? How did you escape?" Chameil demanded.

"I didn't exactly escape. She guided me to the Gate. Her name is Sabnock. She is a great commander of many Legions. And she has all these tattoos on her arms and legs..." Lymineah's small wings began fluttering wildly in her excitement, lifting her several inches off the floor. "And...and she has muscles thiiiis big," she exclaimed spreading her arms as wide as possible. "Oh, and her sword is as tall as you...only taller...and shiny...very shiny...and she kept the others from eating me."

Chameil was stunned by Lymineah's ramblings. Normally, the small Dominion was very subdued, like most of her kind.

"Lymineah, hush!" Chameil ordered, motioning for her to settle back onto the floor before she fell. Dominions weren't capable of flying. Their wings were too small to support their weight. "This demoness — I've heard of her. She is indeed a great warrior. The Principalities and Angels fear her, with good reason. Our Army has never won a single battle against her Legions. Why would she help you?"

Chameil began to pace, unsettled by the news. Demons were incapable of compassion or feelings — except for lust. Their lust was legendary. What was this Sabnock up to?

"She wanted me to deliver a message to you. I told her you were my Mistress." Lymineah puffed her chest out proudly.

"A message? What message?"

Lymineah looked nervously around the chamber.

"It's for your ears alone, Mistress."

"No one would dare enter here without my permission. What did she say?"

"Dis wants to end the war. He seeks a truce and wants you to present his offer to our Master."

"A truce?" Chameil stopped pacing and returned to Lymineah. "A truce? Impossible! You must have misunderstood. Dis is too proud to offer such a thing."

"It's true! Sabnock said Lilith has given him an ultimatum. Either he ends the war or she'll leave him and return to our Master. It's ridiculous that he would accept a truce because of that."

Chameil smiled.

But very smart! It's the one thing that could get Him to agree.

Few would understand the consequences of such a threat. She did.

"Ah! Well now, that makes sense."

"I don't understand. Isn't that what our Master wants? Lilith's return?"

"In the beginning. But, I doubt if he would accept her back now. She would wreak havoc here. The Fallen can never return to the Overworld. They have been forever changed."

23

"But Lilith isn't a Fallen. She was human."

"Even more reason not to bring her back. Dis made her a demon. The change is irreversible. She can't survive here. No demon can."

"Then why are we still fighting this war? It makes no sense. Dis must know that. Her threat is worthless."

"Actually, it's the best weapon Lilith has and the only one the Twins would take seriously. Lilith knows she can't come back. Dis knows she can't, and the Master knows that she can't. Think about it for a while."

Chameil patted Lymineah's shoulder empathetically. *You'll figure it out,* she thought, amused by the Dominion's confusion. It would distract Lymineah from worrying too much about her punishment for being disobedient...and she would be punished. Rules had to be obeyed if order was to be maintained.

"I must contact our Master with the news. It'll be interesting to see his reaction. I'll be back in a while. You are to tell no one about this, ever," Chameil said and disappeared.

Lymineah plopped down on the floor. Her arms rested on her bent knees and her forehead on her arms. Chameil would find her still in this position when she returned.

CHAPTER 5

THE BATTLE CRIES were beginning to fade as more and more warriors fell beneath the onslaught of flashing swords and suffered the punishing blows of spiked bludgeons. Most of the dead or dying were the lower castes of Principalities and Virtues from the Overworld or the hordlings and minions from the Underworld. They were the easiest to destroy. The demons and caste of Powers were different. Minor wounds healed instantly. The more serious took several milliseconds.

Still, if enough injuries were rapidly inflicted on a body, even the most powerful warrior would succumb to the assault. Few actually died during one-on-one conflicts. A minimum of five-to-one was needed if there was any hope of destroying an enemy demon or Power. It was because of this that being outnumbered didn't preclude winning unless the odds were overwhelming.

Sabnock could feel the fire in her blood waning as she continued swinging her sword at one attacker and then countered the blows and strikes from the others. Her warriors were systematically pushing the enemy back into the clouds. It was almost impossible to take a step forward without stumbling over the dead or wounded.

"Forward!" she yelled, her voice booming like rolling thunder. "Keep moving them backward! We fight for Dis and Lilith!"

"For Dis and Lilith!"

"For Dis and Lilith!"

The battle cries spread across the clearing, drowning those of the enemy.

Sabnock parried a sword strike with her shield and jabbed her own sword into the body of a Power. It wasn't a death blow, but it served to distract the warrior long enough for her to shove him aside. Several minions and hordlings pounced on him and began striking relentlessly with their weapons.

Pressing forward, Sabnock focused on one of the remaining three warriors trying to destroy her. He was a Seraphim, which surprised her since most of that hierarchy were inept at fighting. They tended to be more cerebral and were only combative on an intellectual level. This one was different. His skills almost equaled hers. With the other two Powers at his side, he was a real threat.

The unexpected rush of the Power on her left distracted her momentarily. Swinging her sword in a downward sweep, she deflected the sword moving at her left knee. At the same time, she stepped backward, coming in contact with the body of one of her own fallen warriors. Instinctively, she glanced down to make sure she didn't injure him further.

It was all the Seraphim needed. Lunging forward, he plunged his sword into her side. The pain burned like nothing she had ever felt before. No one had ever penetrated her defenses so well. Without thinking, she grabbed the blade and yanked it out, throwing the Seraphim off-guard. As he stumbled backward, Sabnock swung her sword at the second Power, who was trying to take advantage of the situation by cutting her head off.

She twirled, slicing into the back of the first Power. It crumpled to the ground like the other one. By the time her arc returned her to the Seraphim, the distant battle cries had subsided and an eerie silence had taken hold of the clearing.

Sabnock took another backward step, carefully avoiding the wounded imp she had almost tripped over, and looked around her. Thousands of bodies littered the ground. The remaining warriors held their weapons high in the air and chanted:

"For Dis and Lilith! For Dis and Lilith!"

Sabnock raised her own sword and pumped it into the air, a tribute to their victory. She then turned to the Seraphim, who had also been looking at the chaotic scene around him. The hopelessness and sorrow in his pale blue eyes said more than words ever could. All of his comrades either lay fallen around him or had retreated into the clouds.

"This is madness," he muttered. Tears flowed down his cheeks, surprising Sabnock.

"They fought with honor. Why do you cry?" she asked, dropping her shield to check her wound. With her energy level low, it was healing more slowly than usual.

"I cry for their pain and suffering."

"They were warriors. If they have suffered, so have you. What about yours?"

"Mine is of no consequence. It would be selfish to put myself before them."

"Good warriors need good leaders," Sabnock countered. "Good leaders look after themselves first in order to take care of their warriors. You fight well, Seraphim," she said.

"As do you, demoness. Destroy me now so that I may die knowing I served my Master well," he said, lowering his sword.

"I don't kill for the sake of killing. The battle is over. The victory is ours. You are no longer a threat. There's neither need nor honor in destroying you now.

"Besides, you have many wounded to attend to, as do we. Take care of them before the clearing shifts. Both sides have lost too many to the mysteries that lie within the clouds."

The Seraphim again looked around him.

"There isn't much I can do for so many. I'll stay and guard them until my backup comes or the clouds take us."

"Your backup won't be arriving. They too have been destroyed."

"Then I'm all that stands between mine and whatever hides out there."

"You're a fool," Sabnock said.

"Perhaps. These are my people, demoness. It's my duty to protect them. If I'm a fool, I will be an honorable one. Would you be any less of one if you were in my position?"

"I have been one for a long time," she replied while motioning to two of her junior officers to step forward. "This is Duke Valafar, sub-commander of ten of my Legions and Uphir, one of my most trusted physicians. They'll assist you in getting home."

"But Commander..." Valafar protested.

Furious at the interruption, Sabnock backhanded him across the face.

"You dare to challenge me in front of another?" Sabnock questioned coldly, her eyes blazing from barely suppressed rage. "Return to your Legions. I will deal with you later."

Valafar could not conceal his terror.

"My Commander, I meant no disrespect. You misunderstand me."

Realizing he was making the situation worse, Valafar knelt on one knee and bowed his head. "Forgive me, Commander Sabnock. I am battle weary and my thoughts are as cloudy as the mists that surround us. I wish only to serve you faithfully and dutifully."

Seeing an opportunity to turn the situation to her advantage, Sabnock smiled benevolently at Valafar. He was popular among the Legionnaires. Were she to discipline him for a perceived slight while requiring a Legion to assist the enemy, some would question her rationale and her competence as Commander.

Not that they don't anyway...but never too loudly or boldly, she thought before addressing Valafar.

"I understand your weariness. Up until now, you have served me well. I'll overlook your insubordination *this* time. Don't repeat the mistake."

"Never, Commander Sabnock. Upon my word."

"Good. Now, take one Legion and Uphir to collect the bodies of our enemies. You are to take them to the edge of the Zone nearest the Gates and leave them. Afterward, return to camp and await my orders."

"As you wish, Commander. It will be done!"

When Valafar and Uphir left, Sabnock turned her attention back to the Seraphim.

"You are responsible for the safety of my warriors if they encounter your army!"

The Seraphim struck his chest with his right fist.

"You have my word. Why are you doing this? It makes no sense."

"Does any of this?" Sabnock asked, motioning to the bodies around them. "We're duty-bound to serve our masters. Does that mean we must like it?"

The Seraphim hesitated, reluctant to speak what he had felt for eons.

"Your eyes speak what you are unable to say, Seraphim."

"I have a name. It's Gabreolle, son of Gabriel."

"The Archangel. I've heard of him. He was quite brazen in demanding that Lord Dis return Lilith to the Twin."

"He's used to getting his way and is tenacious when performing his duties."

"Then you are indeed of his blood. How is it that the son of an Archangel can be Seraphim? Your society is a caste system."

"Hierarchy can be attained by either parent or by deed. My mother is Seraphim. I inherited Seraphim qualities, therefore I am Seraphim."

And the Archangel skills for fighting. Of all of my adversaries, you inflicted the most damage to my body.

Looking beyond Gabreolle, Sabnock felt uneasy when gray tentacles snaked toward a fallen warrior.

"The clouds are moving," Sabnock said. "Go while you still can. Everyone must be accounted for before the fog takes them."

"Thank you, Commander Sabnock. One question, though. How will we find our way to the Gates? There are no Thrones to guide us and I understand that only a few demons are capable of returning to the Underworld without a guide."

"That's true for the most part. Uphir, however, has a rare skill. He can find his way anywhere."

"Again, I thank you for your generosity. As much as I don't like it, I'm in your debt."

Realizing she had an opportunity to further Dis' cause, Sabnock decided to take a gamble with the Seraphim.

"The debt will be paid if you do me a favor," she offered.

Gabreolle gave her an expectant look but said nothing.

"Do you know the Seraphim Chameil?"

"I know her."

"Tell her of this battle."

"What does she have to do with this?"

"Nothing. Will you tell her?"

"Yes."

"Good. Now go!"

Sabnock sheathed her sword and turned to her Legions.

"Gather our fallen. The clouds are on the move. We must get everyone before any are lost forever."

Seraphim and demoness parted, both hoping they would never meet again.

CHAPTER 6

CHAMEIL NEVER REVEALED what transpired between her and the Twin. Rumors ran rampant. For all their piousness, the inhabitants of the Overworld loved to gossip. Some spoke of a great argument with booming voices rolling like thunder from the inner sanctum of their Master.

Few believed it. Chameil was always soft spoken, even during the most heated of debates. She would never challenge the Master in such a manner. What everyone did know, though, was astounding. The Twin's Army was called back home the next day. Archangel Gabriel was immediately dispatched to meet with the demoness Sabnock. Upon his return, the warriors were discharged from their duties in the Army and instructed to return home. An explanation was never offered and no one dared to ask for one.

* * *

The end of the Great Battle was sowing confusion throughout the population. Chameil spent most of her time helping the battle weary warriors re-integrate into society. Thousands of years of combat couldn't be wiped away by a simple decree to return to their former lives. Mental and emotional problems plagued even the most devoted subject.

Shuffling through the records in front of her, Chameil failed to hear the small wall chimes jingling.

"Mistress?" a timid voice whispered, breaking her concentration.

Chameil looked up to see Lymineah standing a few feet away.

"Ah, Lymineah. I didn't hear you come in. What is it?"

"You have a visitor, Mistress. Seraphim, Gabreolle."

"Gabreolle? Send him in," Chameil said. She had met him once and had heard marvelous stories about his prowess in battle. Watching him stroll into the room, she could believe all of them — not that anyone in the Overworld lied. Truth, however, was exaggerated some.

"Gabreolle! I'm honored. What can I do for you?"

"It is I who am honored, Chameil. I know how busy you have been."

"Yes, but it's a duty I'm happy to perform. We've lost too many in the war.

Motioning for Gabreolle to sit, Chameil pushed the records in front of her aside and leaned forward.

"I'm sure you have a compelling reason to be here," she said.

"Yes. I've come to fulfill a promise I made on the battlefield...to a demon."

"A demon? I must say, you have piqued my curiosity. What is this promise and what does it have to do with me?"

"I can't answer the second question. As for the promise, I gave my word to the demoness Sabnock I would tell you what happened during the last battle between her Legions and our Army. Do you have time to listen?"

"I have all the time in the world," Chameil said.

"Thank you. First, I must tell you we lost that encounter even though we outnumbered our enemy. I have never seen such precision and determination in warriors. I used to believe we were the better fighters but..."

"But you are no longer sure," Chameil finished for him.

"Am I wrong to doubt us?" Gabreolle asked.

"Not as long as you keep it in perspective and learn from it. I am familiar with Sabnock." Chameil saw no need to disclose any other information. "Her reputation as a commander and a warrior is renowned. You're lucky you were not seriously wounded or destroyed."

"It wasn't luck. She spared me and my warriors."

Chameil's eyebrows shot upward. This was indeed surprising. Twice the demoness had shown benevolence and kindness to her enemies.

I must meet this woman, she thought. *Demon or not, she intrigues me.*

"How strange," Chameil said. "Demons aren't known for their compassion."

"Exactly. I've asked myself over and over why she did it. It would have been so easy to destroy all of us. I...I even gave her the opportunity, once I realized we were defeated."

Gabreolle lowered his head, ashamed that he had given in to such weakness. Chameil saw his distress and stood. Walking to where he sat, she put her arms around him.

"There is no shame in accepting truth, Gabreolle. Our Master would expect no less of you. It's time to move on. Now, tell me everything so that I may better understand this demoness."

Gabreolle spent hours describing the battle in graphic detail. Nothing was left out. Tears flowed down his cheeks as he relived the scenes, particularly the final moments of defeat. Chameil listened without interrupting. When he was done, she sensed his overwhelming relief.

"This unburdening was extremely important to you."

"It was. I gave my word."

"And you have fulfilled your promise. Thank you for that."

"One thing I don't understand," Gabreolle said. "Why was it so important to this demoness that you know what happened?"

"I don't know, Gabreolle. She seems to be an anomaly amongst demons. It's common knowledge that demons have only rudimentary emotions. Perhaps hers are more evolved. I'm just grateful that she spared you and the others."

"As am I. I must go. There's still a lot of work to be done. Transitioning back to a peaceful world isn't as easy as I had thought. I'm not sure I'll be able to adapt."

"It will be hard for many of our people. We'll need you to be strong for them."

"Yes. Again, thank you for your time, Chameil."

"I am honored by your presence. My door is always open to you."

Chameil watched the younger Seraphim as he strode from the room. His story was fascinating.

One day, I need to find this Sabnock. If the demons are evolving, there may be hope for them.

It was a comforting thought — but it was never meant to be.

CHAPTER 7

THE BANQUET ROOM was enormous. Dark burgundy silk sheets lay scattered on the ebony stone floor like pools of coagulated blood around a large circular bed positioned in the middle of the great hall. Shadows danced along the walls, created by the fire fountains. They were positioned strategically between the golden pedestals that supported magnificent statues of Dis, Lord of the Underworld.

Writhing bodies, both on the bed and off, performed every sexual act imaginable: fornication, cunnilingus, penetration, masturbation. Nothing was forbidden, as long as the participants consented...and they always consented. Pleasure was the only thing that mattered, at least to most of the guests.

* * *

Lilith was bored. Placing the back of her hand against her mouth, she yawned and then exhaled softly.

"How much longer are you going to let this go on?" she asked, turning to look at Dis.

She wished she could feel the old passion from eons before. He was magnificent to look at. Massive muscles bulged menacingly, even while relaxed. Dark red skin glowed softly, a consequence of the infinite energy emitted by the eternal fires burning throughout the Underworld.

Dis' omnipotence was born from those flames and continued to feed his powers, making him invincible. Still, the most ambitious denizens of the Underworld continued to scheme and plot his overthrow, much to Dis' amusement...and Lilith's.

"Have you grown bored so soon?" Dis asked, running his finger up and down her arm.

"I grew bored a few thousand years ago. Nothing has changed since then."

"You know that's not true," Dis countered. "You have changed. There was once a time when you were insatiable. The mere mention of a party made you wet."

Lilith grimaced, not wanting to be reminded of the early years. She appreciated everything that Dis had taught her and done for her, but now she felt that her life was wasting away. The thought of spending an eternity partying was unimaginable.

"You're right, of course. I long for those days, but nothing will bring them back. Am I so transparent now?"

Dis stopped caressing her arm. Lying on his side next to her, with his head propped on his right hand, he reminded her of a young demon as he fingered the sheets in front of him with his left hand. Rarely did he get nervous, but this small gesture was always a dead giveaway.

"Only to me. I knew this time would eventually come."

Intrigued, Lilith clasped his hand in hers to still its movements. It wasn't good for others to see any signs of weakness, not that she considered his few vulnerabilities weaknesses.

"You knew? How could you know?"

Grinning almost sheepishly, his reddish-brown eyes gleamed with suppressed humor.

"You're an intelligent woman. The smartest I've ever known. Perhaps too smart. That's why I was first attracted to you. It was only a matter of time before you would grow bored here."

Taken off guard by his intuitiveness, Lilith wasn't sure how to respond. "I've surprised you," Dis said and then he laughed, his deep baritone rumbling through the great hall. For a few seconds all activity stopped as everyone turned to see what had amused their Underlord. When he ignored their curious glances, they returned to their pleasures.

"Yes."

"I'm not insensitive, Lily. We've been together a long time. I sense your restlessness and your boredom...not that you're the only one whose been feeling that lately."

"You? You're bored?" Lilith said, stunned.

Again Dis laughed. "Never. I'm not as evolved as you." Pointing to a solitary figure in a darkened corner, he grimaced. "Sabnock doesn't hide her feelings as well as she used to."

Lilith stared at the demoness, only now conscious of the dark waves of energy radiating from her direction.

"Have you talked to her?"

Dis shrugged. "What's there to talk about? Even though the war is over, I still need to maintain my Legions. Sabnock is my best commander. I need her to maintain discipline among the warriors."

"That's ridiculous, Dis, and you know it. You have many competent commanders. Surely they can keep your warriors entertained without Sabnock. You know it's never good to be so dependent on just one person."

"My servants are solely dependent on me. I see no problem in trusting my Legions to Sabnock. Besides, she has no desire to challenge me as Underlord."

"Then she's even smarter than I thought. I don't know why anyone would want your position. Always wondering who's scheming and plotting..."

"That's one of the benefits," Dis said and chuckled, swinging his arm in an arc to encompass the entire room. "Most of them want what I have. They fawn and grovel, hoping that I will notice them, all the while planning my demise. It's quite entertaining."

"No wonder you're not bored," Lilith said. "Perhaps if you experienced what Sabnock is feeling...what I'm feeling...you'd be more understanding."

"Lily. Even if I were more *understanding*, what can I do?"

"I don't know. Call her over. Let's see what she wants?"

Dis shrugged, but Lilith knew he would do as she asked. Dis always did what Lilith asked. She was his one great weakness, not to mention that she was the only demon who could satisfy his burning lust.

"As you wish, my dear," he said and motioned to one of his servants to come near. "Tell Commander Sabnock I wish to speak to her."

Scurrying away, the servant navigated through the mass of twisting bodies to Sabnock's table. The demoness glanced toward Dis and Lilith, stood, and strode purposefully to the bed they were reclining in.

"You wish my services, My Lord?" she asked, bowing slightly at the waist.

"No," Dis replied. "Only an answer to a question Lilith has posed."

"Mistress?"

"Are you unhappy, Sabnock?" Lilith asked.

CHAPTER 8

SABNOCK BARELY CONTAINED her surprise at the question. Lilith rarely interacted with warriors. Some mistook her distant attitude as snobbery, but Sabnock knew better. Her Mistress was a cerebral person. She was more interested in knowledge than war.

"I...don't understand what you mean, Mistress."

"Come, Commander. You're an intelligent woman. You know exactly what I mean. Are you unhappy? Or is 'bored' a better word?"

"I have plenty to do. The Legions take up a lot of my time."

"That wasn't my question."

Glancing at Dis, Sabnock was surprised by his intense stare. He was as much interested in her answer as Lilith.

"There are times." *Every minute, as a matter of fact,* she thought.

"Like every minute," Lilith said and then laughed at the surprise on Sabnock's face. "No, I didn't read your thoughts, Sabnock. You have lost your zest."

"I'm sorry it's that obvious, Mistress. I will remove myself from the party," Sabnock offered, misunderstanding Lilith.

"That's not what this is about, Sabnock. Dis and I are concerned about you. You're too valuable to us as a warrior and as a friend." Dis' cough caused the two women to look at the Underlord. "You know it's true so stop that," Lilith chastised teasingly.

"Is this how you talk to me in front of one of my commanders?" he growled menacingly.

"Men, you've got to love them," Lilith said, and then remembered that Sabnock preferred women. "Or not! Is there something else you want to do? You made commander before the Great Battle. Perhaps a change would do you good."

Sabnock knew this was the moment of truth. She could either take her chances by honestly answering Lilith's question or continue stagnating in her present position. Bowing her head, she was undecided.

*I am pledged to serve them. It would be breaking my oath to ask...*The thought made her shiver. Breaking her oath was unimaginable. She would destroy herself before doing such a thing.

"You hesitate," Dis interrupted. "Is there?"

"I serve you, My Lord and Mistress," Sabnock said, and snapped to attention.

"There's your answer, Lily," Dis said, happy to have resolved the issue.

"Yes," she agreed. "But not to my question. I want the truth, Commander. As your mistress, I demand that you answer me honestly."

Sabnock had no choice but to do as she was ordered.

"I want to go to the mortal world," she replied reluctantly.

Dis' eyebrows shot up and he smiled benevolently.

"That's it? That's all? By all means. Take time off and go play," he said happily.

"I don't think that's what she means, Dis, and you know it."

Sighing, the Underlord shook his head. Lilith knew he was frustrated. Patting his hand, she said one word.

"Later." It was a promise he understood and he immediately cheered up. "What would you do there?" Lilith asked.

"Live! I would live!"

"Live how?"

"As a human mortal."

"Impossible," Dis declared. "You're a demon. There's no way you can be changed into one of them."

"I know, My Lord, but I can try. I feel what they feel, pain, sorrow, lust. They're really not so different than us except they are still in flux. They constantly battle with each other. I could put my sword to good use."

"But you can't be killed. At least not by a human," Dis said. *If only it were true here,* he thought, remembering the tens of thousands of demons that had been cremated. Prior to the Great Battle, even he had thought his demons were beyond Death's grasp.

"No, but I believe Death would allow me to experience the sensation...if you asked."

"Why would I do that? Death has stolen enough of my subjects already. Besides, you are my best commander. It would be crazy to let you go on such a foolish escapade."

"I understand, My Lord. It was only a thought," Sabnock replied, her enthusiasm waning. "If you will excuse me, My Lord, Mistress..."

"I will not, Commander," Lilith said and then turned to Dis. "Let her go, Dis."

44

"What?" he bellowed. When the room grew silent, he glared at the nervous guests. "Get out!" he yelled. Within seconds, the room was emptied. "You ask a lot, Lily," Dis said, ignoring Sabnock.

This should be interesting, Sabnock thought, intrigued at the battle of wills taking place in front of her.

"Let her go. She is of no use to you now."

"I..."

"Be quiet, Sabnock. This is between Dis and I."

Sabnock knew better than to disobey. Taking two steps back, she waited to see who would win this battle of wills.

"Think about it. No matter how good a commander she was or is, her heart isn't here anymore. Can't you see that she is now useless in her present position? Let her go. At least she can continue to practice her skills with the mortals."

"They would stand no chance fighting her."

"If she wants to live amongst them, then she's going to have to live like them. If Death is willing to help her accomplish her desires, why wouldn't you? You could always ask her to come back if you really needed her."

"Ask! *Ask*?" There was no doubt the Underlord was appalled at the thought.

"Never mind, dear. It's just a thought. Do this for me. I know what she's feeling. She is dying on the inside."

You're as bored as I am, Sabnock thought. *What about you? What will you do?*

"Is this really what you want?" Dis asked Sabnock. "To forsake your people and your homeworld?"

"I'm not forsaking them, My Lord. I just need something more than this."

"Then go! You are absolved of your oath."

That's it? Just like that, I'm released from my duties? Sabnock wasn't sure whether to be overjoyed or insulted.

"I suggest you take advantage of Dis' generosity and go, Commander," Lilith said, her voice barely hiding her humor.

"Of course. I am grateful for your kindness. Thank you, My Lord." Turning to look at Lilith, their gazes locked in understanding. "And to you, Mistress."

Lilith gave a slight nod and then turned to her mate.

"I believe we have some business to attend to...a promise...later."

"Yes. Yes we do," he replied, standing and holding out his hand for her to take. "I wish you many battles, Commander."

Sabnock knew she had been dismissed. Placing her right fist over her heart, she bowed at the waist and disappeared. Her journey had begun.

The End of the Great Battle

Warrior Demoness

CHAPTER 1

SHE HAD volunteered for the assignment, just as she had done all of her life. The consummate warrior, death wasn't a stranger to her or to be feared. How does one fear that which will never happen? Once she had commanded fifty legions for her liege.

During the Great Battle, she had lost many demons and minions to the Twin's brigades and never completely recovered from it, perhaps because she never knew where they went when they disappeared. Demons didn't die. At least, that was what she believed.

The Underlord had been grateful for her efforts, but was reluctant to release her from her oath of loyalty. Good commanders, who weren't overly ambitious, were hard to find in the Underworld. Had it not been for the intervention of his wife, Lilith, Sabnock suspected she would still be leading his legions, and *that* would have bored her to death.

Even though Dis maintained a strong force, there were no more great battles left to fight. The feud between the Underlord and his Twin had become more civilized. Neither of them seemed to take much of an interest in mankind nowadays. Each left the fate of humans to their own devices or to the mischief of the two immortals' subjects.

For that, Sabnock was grateful. Being short-sighted, demons and angels tended to focus more on individuals than humanity as a whole. It gave her plenty of opportunities to keep her skills honed and her sanity intact.

* * *

"Sabnock! Get your head out of your ass and get over here!"

Sabnock smirked. Sgt. Wilkins could be such an asshole but he was proficient at his job and a good leader.

"Yes, Sergeant!" she yelled back.

Throwing her rifle over her left shoulder, she loped gracefully over to his position and saluted.

"Reporting as ordered," she declared, knowing her actions would aggravate him.

"How many times have I told you not to salute enlisted men, corporal? Didn't you learn in basic?"

"No sir, Sergeant, sir! That's why I'm still a corporal, sir," she bellowed, standing at attention.

Shaking his head, Wilkins didn't know if she was serious or pulling his leg. One moment she seemed totally incompetent and the next almost brilliant. There was definitely something about her that he couldn't quite figure out, but as long as she did her job, he had no complaints. And Sabnock always did her job when it came to the important matters. Had she shown some ambition, she would have made sergeant a long time ago. It was almost as if she was intentionally sabotaging her chances to rise in rank.

"The C.O. wants someone to check out a small settlement ten clicks to the south. Intelligence says there are several insurgents stashing weapons and explosives in one of the homes."

"And how are we supposed to locate these insurgents, Sarge?" Sabnock asked. It was the right question to ask even though the corporal knew she had the ability to find them if she wanted to. Such were the powers of a demoness when she chose to use them. She had decided not to in order to live a more human existence. Sabnock wanted to experience their feelings and emotions as much as was demonly possible. It was the only thing that gave meaning to her life now.

"That's your problem, Sabnock. The C.O. doesn't want questions. Only results. He knows you've been doing this long enough to get the job done right. Why you keep pissing him off so much is beyond me, but that's your business. Now, get a move on it."

"Yes, sir."

Saluting, she pivoted in true military form and trotted off to see who would volunteer for the mission. She knew most of the troops were gung-ho so it wouldn't be hard to get a dozen soldiers to accompany her. Everyone who knew her believed she had some magic charm that would keep them safe. Sabnock could have. She chose not to. Still, it was interesting watching everyone around her behave confidently, especially knowing *that* belief was the real reason for their luck.

The area had been secured three weeks earlier. Now, except for the occasional trusted villager wandering by, no one came within a quarter mile of the encampment without being checked. Security had to be tight to protect the troops.

"Hey there, Sabby!" yelled a deep voice as she approached the brown camouflaged tents scattered near a partially destroyed building.

A tall, lanky soldier with sandy blond hair waved at her. Sabnock smiled. Lanny's voice didn't fit his looks. Baritones were supposed to be big stocky men, not scrawny boys like him. He was a good soldier, though, and had a nice personality.

"Sarge wants us to check a village nearby," she said. "There have been reports of insurgents in the area."

"Now? We just got back from a field op."

"That was eight hours ago. Plenty of time to rest."

"For you, maybe, but the rest of us need more than a few hours to recoup," Lanny grumbled.

"Well, the Sarge didn't say when we have to leave so tell the guys to get a couple more hours of sleep and report to me at 1300 hours. I'll go ahead and requisition the supplies we'll need. I imagine we'll be away for a few days."

"Thanks, Sabby."

Sabnock knew her buddies were exhausted from a two week stint in the foothills near Sarhadd, a small village in the Wakhan Corridor of the country. Because of its proximity to Pakistan and China and the rugged terrain, it was the perfect location for insurgents to pass unnoticed between Afghanistan and the adjacent countries. Sabnock and her unit had been in the area for eight months, trying to eliminate the resistance.

During that time she had sustained several injuries, but nothing serious enough to cause her to be transitioned out. Unfortunately, three of her comrades had been killed, something she regretted deeply, knowing she could have prevented the loss had she chosen to use her skills as a demon. Her decision not to intervene, however, was not a real problem. In order to understand humanity, she had to play the part the best she could. That meant letting fate have its way no matter how painful the consequences.

Shaking her head, she tried to push the troubling memories aside. Reminiscing was always painful, but it kept everything in perspective – or at least helped, in a perverted sort of way. One memory in particular would haunt her forever. It was the worst decision she had ever made in her many lives.

Walking over to a stack of crates, she slid down to the ground and rested her forearms on her bent knees. The sun beat mercilessly down on everything, causing everyone but the guards to stay in their tents. Sabnock loved these moments. It was the only time everything seemed to stop and it reminded her of home, a place she hadn't returned to in several hundred years.

There was nothing and no one in the Underworld waiting for her. She had been a loner for as long as she could remember, but once...once. Burying her head in her hands, she closed her eyes and let her thoughts wander back to a time when she had been loved, not as a demon by a demon. but as a human by another.

51

CHAPTER 2

IT BEGAN WHEN the messenger appeared at the entrance of her tent.

"Lt. Lynara, sir. Queen Boudicea sends her regards and requests your presence."

She remembered smiling when he finished delivering the message. Requests from the supreme leader were actually orders, but it made the queen appear more accessible.

"When and where is this meeting?" she asked, watching him fidget nervously a few feet away.

"Tonight, after the third watch takes over. Her majesty wishes you to meet her at the old ruins near the druids' circle."

"As she commands," Lynara said obediently. "Please tell her I'll be there."

The messenger nodded respectfully and departed.

Lynara called to her servant to bring her hot water. She would take a bath and dress appropriately for her meeting with the supreme commander. That was what was expected of her.

* * *

Five candlemarks later, dressed in her best *breches*, a doeskin slipover sleeveless tunic with a wide belt, leather boots and matching cloak, she strolled through the darkness toward the ruins. Occasionally, one of the Celtic guards challenged her, but it was merely a formality. Everyone knew the lieutenant was favored by their Queen. Few were willing to alienate the young officer. Besides, the prowess of Lt. Lynara as a warrior was legendary. Only the bravest and most intelligent became officers, unless they were from wealth or royalty.

A few campfires burned dimly around the encampment. Shadows danced eerily amongst the trees as the flames flickered in the cold winds blowing off the moors. The druids' circle was dark and quiet. It had been abandoned for a long time, when the Romans decided to exterminate them and their followers.

Looking around, Lynara discovered the site was vacant.

Good, she thought. Lynara loved the night. It reminded her of home, especially when the fires burned brightly. The dancing flames brought back the nostalgia felt by those who had been away from home too long, but knew it would be even longer before they returned.

"Good evening, Lieutenant," spoke a woman's voice from the darkness.

"Your Highness," Lynara said, nodding her head respectfully.

"Thank you for coming."

"I am always at your command, My Queen."

Two women stepped from the shadows. The first, Lynara recognized instantly. No one could mistake the large woman with the flaming red hair. Boudicea was

53

impressive as both a woman and a queen, but as a warrior she was magnificent.

The second woman was smaller and appeared a few years older. Her long dark hair was braided into one large strand and draped over her right shoulder. Black eyes gleamed brilliantly in the moonlight. Petite, she was dwarfed by Boudicea. Still, her bearing was enough to tell Lynara that the stranger was quite capable of handling most situations.

* * *

"This is Constance. She is a historian." Boudicea nudged Constance forward with her hand.

Lynara was surprised. The battlefield was no place for scholars.

"A historian, highness?"

"Yes. She has come to write our story. It's important our descendants know the truth about us and how this war started."

"Truth is illusive and rarely told accurately, My Queen."

Boudicea nodded.

"That's why I've asked you to come. Of all my commanders, you are the one I trust the most to tell how we got to this point."

"Me? I'm a warrior, not a scholar. Wouldn't it be better to get one of the tribal elders to tell your story? They are familiar with the art of storytelling and know more of your history."

"Pffft!" snorted the queen. "They embellish everything. Even I, who have been there, don't recognize the events when they tell their stories. No, Lieutenant, I want someone who doesn't have the imagination to make up stories. I mean that as a compliment, Lynara."

The use of her name surprised Lynara. Never had the queen referred to her by anything except her rank.

"Of course. I am yours to command, My Queen," she replied hesitantly.

"Good. Now take Constance to your tent and tell her everything you know to be true. The Romans are on the march and will be here within a fortnight. I want her gone by then."

"One question, My Queen. There's much I know and a lot I've heard. Should I tell her the latter?

"Tell her everything. She'll know what's true and what's not. Answer her questions as you would if it were I asking. Now, go. I'm late for a meeting with my generals."

* * *

Constance watched the Celtic queen and her young lieutenant with interest. It was obvious there was a great affection between them, even though it was unspoken. Both had red hair, not uncommon in the Celts. The two women were a contrast. Boudicea was big-boned with coarse features and a wild and unmanageable mane, while the lieutenant was tall and muscular. Her hair was long and wavy with an unusual shine. Although it was cold, the warrior's arms were bare, revealing tattooed flames on both of her biceps. Even in the darkness they glowed brightly.

She must be very confident, Constance thought. *An enemy would find her an easy target.*

The historian also noticed that the woman spoke without the usual Celtic brogue and that her Gaelic was flawless. Boudicea, who had been born to aristocracy, didn't speak as well.

Bowing slightly, Lynara motioned for Constance to go ahead. After touching her fingertips to her forehead in a salute to her queen, the lieutenant followed the historian. Boudicea laughed quietly. The gesture was unique to Lynara and had always amused Boudicea. Several of her generals thought it disrespectful and occasionally objected. Boudicea knew otherwise and forbade them to say anything to the young warrior.

CHAPTER 3

BACK IN HER tent, Lynara invited Constance to sit on a small chest near the bed. Although her accommodations were cramped, it was roomy enough for the two women to be moderately comfortable.

"What is it you wish to know?"

"You don't waste time, do you?" Constance asked, tipping her head slightly as she made eye contact with the young officer.

"I'm a warrior. Time is precious to those who may die at any minute."

"I imagine it is. Before we begin, tell me something about yourself, lieutenant."

Lynara stared at the historian for several seconds. The last thing she wanted was to talk about was herself.

"I thought you were to write about our queen."

"That is my intent, of course, but to understand her, I must understand those who serve her."

"Understanding me won't help you to know Boudicea. It will only take up valuable time."

Constance smiled.

"You're a philosopher."

"If a warrior makes it to my age, he or she can't help but be one. It makes what we do and say meaningful."

"And how old are you?" Constance asked, guessing that the young woman could be no older than three decades.

"In years or in life experiences?"

"Let's start with years. Then we can discuss your experiences."

Lynara hesitated before answering. Were she to tell Constance the truth, it would sound too incredible to believe. Still, it would be fun to watch her expression. The woman was too...

Too what? she asked herself. Self-assured? Confident?

"I have been around for a few decades." She prevaricated after deciding Constance would be an interesting challenge.

Constance didn't miss the subtleness of the answer, but decided not to press Lynara further. She had almost two weeks to unravel the mystery. Instead, she focused on her original goal.

"Well, how about telling me how this war started?"

"Didn't Boudicea tell you?"

"Yes, but I want to know what others believe. One person's story isn't entirely dependable."

"If Boudicea told you, then it is. She always speaks the truth."

"Then she's rare indeed. My experience has shown few people always speak the truth."

Lynara shrugged. She couldn't argue that point. "Where do you want me to begin?"

"Perhaps you can tell me what happened to Prasutagus?"

"The king? He was a great warrior. The Romans were wise to keep him on the throne. It's a shame they showed less wisdom with Boudicea."

Constance nodded her head sagely.

"Yes. She would have been better as an ally than an enemy."

"Had they not tried to humiliate her or raped her daughters, she would have been less of a threat."

"No one should endure that. Nero's generals gave him poor advice. He should have known better."

Taking her knife from her sheath, Lynara examined the edge carefully, testing its razor sharp edge with her thumb. It was more a habit than a necessity.

"Rome's generals are known for their greed – not their intelligence. The only thing they know is power and money," Lynara said, not looking up. "The Iceni were forced from their lands and then tortured because they couldn't pay the ridiculous assessments with which Rome burdened them."

"It's a common mistake that humans make," Constance replied.

Her use of the word *humans* caught Lynara's attention and she glanced toward the entrance curtain to see if any of the guards were within hearing distance. All officers had at least two guards stationed at the openings to prevent unauthorized entry. Seeing they were talking quietly together, she turned to the historian.

"Who are you?"

Realizing her mistake, Constance made eye contact and held the officer's gaze for several seconds. Finally deciding not to challenge the lieutenant, she lowered her eyes.

"An historian, nothing more."

"I find that hard to believe," Lynara retorted.

Constance shrugged.

"Believe what you will. We're wasting time. Tell me what else you know."

Lynara suspected there was more to the historian than she was saying, but decided not to press her further. Her instincts told her she was dealing with someone quite capable of holding her own in a verbal duel.

"Like I said, the Romans tried to humiliate our queen. They stripped her naked and tortured her while her people were made to watch. Then the soldiers took her two daughters and raped them in front of Boudicea, hoping to break her will. Obviously they miscalculated her inner strength."

"Obviously. What was her crime that they were so brutal?"

"Her crime?"

Lynara snorted and threw the knife at a nearby wooden chest. Sticking in the wood, it vibrated back and forth.

"Her crime was being loved. Her husband left her as partial heir to his estate instead of leaving everything to Nero. Roman law requires all possessions of the dead pass to the Emperor. Prasutagus thought he would insure their safety by naming Boudicea and his daughters as co-heirs to his estate."

"That wasn't very smart considering the Roman obsession for obedience."

"I believe his mind was damaged by all of the battles he had fought and then the embarrassment of having to bow to Roman law. During his last years, he acted strangely. His servants said he would wake up screaming in the night. He rarely spoke and at times would suddenly burst into tears. Everyone was afraid he had gone insane. Perhaps that's why he defied Roman law."

"It's a common problem among warriors. I've seen many who act that way. I do believe their experiences unbalance the mind, much like a hard blow to the head."

Lynara nodded. She too had seen it happen many times.

"Yes."

"How did Boudicea escape?"

"The Romans, in their arrogance, released her. After all, she was only a woman. She rescued her daughters and fled to the hills. Her people rallied around her, one-hundred thousand strong, and she has made her torturers pay dearly for their atrocities. She put fear in the hearts of her enemies when she destroyed Londinium. There wasn't a Roman left alive when we departed."

Standing, Constance walked over to pull the knife from the chest. Returning it to Lynara, she sat back down.

"I have heard she is heartless and takes no prisoners."

"She fights a just cause. Sometimes it takes cruelty to achieve that goal."

"The end justifying the means."

"The means justifying the end," Lynara said. An ancient exhaustion overwhelmed her.

Humans waste so much of their lives. I fear they will never grow beyond their petty squabbles.

"We should continue this tomorrow," she said. "It's late and I have an early meeting with my men. You can sleep on the bed."

"Where will you sleep?"

"On a blanket, on the ground. I'm a warrior. It won't kill me."

Knowing it was useless to argue, Constance stood and removed her outer layer of clothing, aware that the lieutenant watched her every move.

"Do you like women, Lieutenant?" she asked boldly, giving Lynara an impish grin.

"I've had my share," Lynara answered, not intimidated by the question or the woman. Indeed, Constance was extremely attractive and well-endowed. "And you?"

"I've had my share," the historian replied in a teasing tone. "But not tonight. I'm too tired."

Lynara laughed. Their time together was going to be very interesting.

CHAPTER 4

FOR THE NEXT two weeks, Lynara and Constance were inseparable. The lieutenant escorted her around the camp, introducing her to others who were more familiar with the events leading up to Boudicea's incarceration and torture. She wanted to make sure that Constance had as much information as possible for her records.

"Do you always take this much interest in your charges?" Constance asked.

"Not always – but then I don't always have such interesting assignments. I'll have to thank My Queen when I see her."

Constance smiled, her cheeks dimpling.

"Me too."

* * *

Neither was sure at what point their relationship shifted from professional to personal. One moment they were talking quietly in Lynara's tent about Roman policies, and the next, they were in each other's arms, both of them kissing as if it would be their last kiss. When they pulled apart, they stared into each other's eyes and smiled almost shyly. It was then they both realized something had been missing from their lives.

That night, they made love. Afterward, they spent hours talking about almost everything, with the exception of themselves. Neither of them wanted to ruin the intimate moment by revealing their darkest secrets. The remaining days passed effortlessly. Too quickly, their time was up.

* * *

Lying beneath the furs, Lynara held Constance firmly against her breasts. Neither spoke. Hours of lovemaking had left them exhausted, but contented. Only the specter of tomorrow's battle haunted their happiness.

"You're thinking about tomorrow," Constance whispered.

"You've known me only two weeks and already you read my mind?"

"I've known you a lifetime."

"A short one, then," Lynara teased.

"True."

"Well, you're right. The Romans are camped a half-day's march from here. We leave at dawn."

"Then we have only a few hours left. Let's use them wisely."

Lynara needed no further encouragement. Rolling Constance on her back, she leaned down and stared longingly into the black eyes of her lover.

"What took you so long to come into my life?" Her voice was husky with emotion.

"I've been around forever. Where have you been?" Constance whispered back, reaching up to stroke the suntanned cheek of her warrior.

"It appears we've wasted a lot of time then."

Leaning down, Lynara kissed Constance, letting her lips move tenderly against her lover's. The contact was gentle, almost tentative, as if asking for permission to continue. Constance felt like she was being branded. Her lips were on fire when Lynara touched them with the tip of her tongue. Lynara's hands lingered at Constance's breasts and then slid down to her stomach.

"You're hands are always so hot," Constance said and groaned.

"Only when I'm with you. You make me burn with desire."

Reaching down, Lynara caressed the dark curly hair covering Constance's mound. Fingers moved playfully through the hair, causing the historian to shift restlessly. Fluid flowed freely, but couldn't cool the hot fingers sliding between her lips to sample the sleek, velvety warmth hiding just beneath the soft curls. Running her tongue down Constance's cheek, Lynara stopped at her throat and nipped at the tender skin at the base of her neck.

"I feel like devouring you." Pulling slightly away, Lynara's hot gaze met her lover's. It was the first time Constance had really looked deeply into her warrior's eyes. The passion blazed so brightly, she swore she saw flames dancing in the dark brown pupils. Blinking, she realized she had never really noticed the unusual color before and couldn't imagine why she had thought Lynara had green eyes.

"Something bothers you, my love?" Lynara asked, frowning slightly.

"You bother me," Constance gasped, "but in a good way."

Lynara grinned.

"Good. Shall I continue?"

"Oh, yes. By all means."

Lowering her head, she again nipped the sensitive area on Constance's neck.

"You taste...salty."

"I've noticed you like salt," Constance said, enjoying the heated lips.

"Uh huh. Now hush. You're distracting me."

Constance would have replied if she hadn't felt a strange heat between her legs. Fingers played erratically between her warm, slick lips, first moving slowly and then speeding up. When they began to dip gently into her vulva, she felt as if her whole body was burning up and wasn't sure if she was experiencing pleasure or pain.

"Pleasure," Lynara whispered against her ear. "There is never pain in true lovemaking."

Constance could feel her eyes rolling back in her head. Gasping, she was barely aware of her hips thrusting upward to the beat of the fingers driving in and out. Lynara's other hand caressed and massaged her breasts, then shifted to her ribs and stomach, rubbing them in a slow, circular motion before moving back to the breasts.

Lips nibbled on earlobes and neck and then down to hardened nipples. Lynara took one between her teeth and tugged on it before swirling her tongue around the areola. Constance could barely control the urge to scream, but knowing two guards stood outside the tent gave her strength to suppress it. Biting her lower lip, she moaned, her head moving back and forth.

Lynara could feel Constance stiffen as wave after wave of pleasure coursed through the warm body beneath her. Finally, Constance arched her back, groaned loudly and then collapsed, sweating pouring down her body and dripping onto the cot.

"Are you alright?" Lynara asked, resting her cheek on the heaving breasts.

"Barely," Constance groaned, trying to catch her breath.

Smiling, the warrior let her entire weight settle on her lover and wrapped her arms around the slender body beneath her. Snuggling in, she sighed and relaxed as a hand began gently stroking her hair.

"When do you have to go?"

Eyes closed, Lynara didn't want to think about it.

"Soon," she whispered against the bare skin next to her lips.

Frowning, Constance suddenly felt uneasy.

"This is it, isn't it? This is all we will have."

Raising her head, Lynara stared into the black eyes of the first woman she had ever loved. Constance met the gaze and frowned. Green eyes, the color of sea-foam, stared back.

I must be imagining things, she thought.

"Can you tell the future?" Lynara teased. In her heart she knew Constance was right. Their time together was over.

"No, it's just a feeling. Am I wrong?"

She hoped Lynara would say yes, but all she did was shrug.

"Who can say? I'm no more a seer than you. What happens, happens," Lynara said philosophically.

Not wanting to ruin the moment, Constance nodded and pulled Lynara close. There was only a little time left. Exhausted, they fell asleep, their bodies interlocked in a warm but gentle embrace.

A candlemark later, one of the guards awoke the lieutenant and motioned toward the tent entrance. The first rays of sunlight peeked over the horizon, turning the sky a deep orange. The color reminded Lynara of her homeland. Rising quietly, she stared at the sleeping figure and smiled sadly. She kissed Constance on the lips, grabbed her clothes and left, unable to look back for fear of giving in to her desire to stay.

* * *

Constance was cold and she shifted slightly. Her body missed the familiar warmth that had shielded her from the cool night air. Opening her eyes slowly, she saw her warrior walking away. Wanting to call out, she smothered the urge with her right fist and settled back down, hoping Lynara wouldn't turn and see her misery. She knew it would make the parting more difficult. Her heart felt on fire, the pain so real she thought she was dying.

I could make you stay, she thought, but knew it would bring a worse death than dying. It would kill their love. *I never said I love you.*

* * *

The lieutenant stopped outside the tent and quickly put on her clothes. She knew the moment Constance woke up. Her body was so in tune with the human that she even felt the same pain. Placing her hand over her chest, she closed her eyes, tipped her head back and gritted her teeth. Her two guards looked nervously at each other.

"Are you not well?" one dared to ask.

"I'm fine, Faolin. Come, our Queen awaits us."

Trotting toward the distant hillside, her thoughts were torn between the approaching battle and the woman she had left behind.

CHAPTER 5

CONSTANCE FELT the fatal blow as if she were the one stabbed. Rushing from the tent she ran toward the distant battlefield. It took over two candlemarks, but she never slowed her pace. Time was of the essence if she was to be with Lynara during her last moments. The moans of the dying could be heard long before she saw the carnage from atop a small hillock.

Constance stared at the devastation before her. Tens of thousands of men, women and children lay dead or dying. Roman or Celt, it made no difference. Death didn't care. It welcomed all gladly. Rushing down the hill, she saw a familiar form staggering toward her.

"Faolin!" she cried, catching the wounded man as he collapsed. "Where is Lieutenant Lynara?"

Eyes glazed with pain, Faolin focused on the woman holding him up.

"Historian?" he asked, his eyes barely able to make out her face.

"Yes, it's me, Constance. Where is Lynara?"

Moving his arm painfully, he pointed to a stack of bodies several hundred paces away. Constance lowered him to the ground.

"Be still, Faolin. I'll be back soon."

The Celt could only nod.

Running toward the pile of bodies, she was appalled at the mutilation around her. Severed arms and legs lay everywhere. Bodiless heads stared at her accusingly. Headless bodies lay crumpled, their arms outstretched as if searching for something that wasn't there.

Trying not to step on any of the remains, she hunted frantically until she spotted the blood-stained body of her lover. Falling to her knees, Constance gently gathered Lynara into her arms, holding her tightly against her breast. The bright red hair flowed across her arms like rivers of blood.

"Lynara? It's me. Come back to me, my love," she pleaded, tears racing down her cheeks. Dark clouds moved across the sky and thunder rolled ominously.

The gods are angry, she thought.

Lynara heard the call and felt torn between the vow she had made thousands of years before and the need to be with the one person who had shown her true love. Opening her eyes, she stared into tear-filled eyes and smiled painfully.

"I knew you would come," she whispered and then winced. To understand life as a mortal, Lynara had chosen to experience everything associated with it, including the pains of her injuries and their consequences. Only the knowledge that she would soon be reborn gave her the strength and courage to endure dying – until this moment. Now, she had to choose between death and happiness. It wasn't an easy choice.

"I waited for you."

"You had better," Constance threatened, trying to ease her lover's passing. There was no doubt Lynara had suffered mortal injuries. "What happened?"

Although the question was directed at Lynara's battle, the warrior pretended to misunderstand.

"Always the historian!" she teased. "My Queen was surr..."

Lynara gasped as fire burned through her gut. She would have to talk quickly. "...sur...rounded by Romans. We fought our way to her side. She was badly wounded but we man...managed to secure her escape."

"You stayed behind to make it happen, didn't you?" Constance accused.

"We stayed."

Looking around, the historian smiled sadly. There were no Celt bodies within thirty paces. She could easily imagine the magnificent battle Lynara had fought.

"So I see," she said knowingly, torn between pride for her warrior and sorrow for the sacrifice of their future.

* * *

Lynara was cold. She knew time was short. If she didn't decide now, it would be too late. She could join Constance and know all that love had to offer or she could die. It should have been easy, but it wasn't. Life meant revealing her greatest secret and she wasn't sure how Constance would feel about her then. There was also the problem of aging. She hated the thought of watching Constance grow old and frail and eventually die. Human life was so short. Demons normally lived forever.

Making up her mind, she reached up to brush the tears from her lover's cheeks.

"I must go now," she whispered, her brown eyes reflecting her sorrow.

They're brown now, Constance thought, momentarily confused. Again she saw flames dancing hotly within their depths. Giving a slight shake of the head, she kept the eye contact, knowing it was essential she hold on to every precious moment.

"I know." Her eyes flooded with more tears.

"Don't cry. We'll meet in another life."

"I prefer this one."

"Me too, but it isn't meant to be."

Death crept closer and for a moment, Lynara panicked. She had died a thousand times before but had never experienced fear.

I can stop this! her mind cried out. *Don't throw away a lifetime of happiness!* it screamed.

"I can't do this!" she groaned aloud, the pain of leaving greater than the pain of dying.

"Do what?" Constance asked, lowering her voice to a soft whisper.

Shaking her head, Lynara didn't answer. Her decision had been made long ago. Two weeks with Constance wasn't enough to break her vow, no matter how wonderful it had been.

It's not two weeks! part of her argued. *It's a lifetime. What use is a vow if it destroys you? Can't you make her happy for the short time she has? You will always be a warrior, but love rarely comes more than once in a lifetime, even a demon's.*

* * *

"Lynara? What is it? What can't you do?"

"Dying! I can't die!"

"There are some things we can't control, my love."

"For some," Lynara replied mysteriously.

Constance frowned, thinking Lynara was delirious. Neither spoke, unsure what to say. Finally, Lynara broke the silence.

"Don't bury me in the ground. I must be burned."

Forcing back a sob, Constance nodded.

"You will have the biggest fire anyone has ever seen. A warrior's funeral," she promised.

"Thank you," Lynara said, feeling Death's grip tightening. "I love you so much. It was a glorious two weeks. I'll miss you."

"I'll miss you too, my love, but we'll be together again. I promise."

"I know," the demoness said, smiling faintly. "Until then, be happy."

"I can't!" cried Constance, clutching Lynara tightly, unable to stay strong. "I can't! Don't leave me!" she begged, hating herself for her weakness at Lynara's last moments.

The demoness heard the anguish and relented, but it was too late. Death had arrived to claim It's prize.

"I'm sorry!" she gasped as her body stiffened. "I...should have...chosen...you."

Not sure what she meant, Constance sobbed uncontrollably. Several Celtic women and a few soldiers surrounded her, wanting to offer comfort but unwilling to disturb the grieving woman. They knew the lieutenant and mourned the loss. Finally, one leaned down and touched Constance's shoulder

"We'll prepare her body," the old woman offered.

"No!" Constance snapped. "I'm sorry. No. I'll do it. Please prepare the pyre for her. It was her wish."

Gesturing for the others to get started, the woman remained standing next to the historian, not sure what else to do.

"Faolin," Constance said, as an afterthought.

"We have him. He'll recover with time."

"And the Queen?"

"She escaped."

Constance nodded and then turned her attention back to her warrior. Death was no stranger to her. One didn't live thousands of years without losing loved ones. Time never healed the pain but it had taught her to accept the inevitable and to deal with it. Pushing aside her feelings of loss, she looked at the fallen warrior with the eyes of an historian instead of a lover. The time for grieving would come later.

"It's as if she were sleeping," she murmured.

"She was the bravest of our warriors. She stayed behind to give our queen time to escape," the woman said.

"She could do no less. She was a Celt," Constance replied.

"Ummm."

The historian gave the woman a questioning look.

"What is it?"

"Lieutenant Lynara wasn't a Celt."

"Not a...I thought.. well, never mind. I was obviously wrong. Where was she from? I want to make sure my records are correct and then notify her family."

"She hasn't any family, and no one knows where she comes from. Except maybe Queen Boudicea."

"No one? She never talked about her life? Her family?"

"She never talked about anything from her past. Whenever anyone asked, she would say her past was a story best untold. We understood and respected her wishes."

"Then I will ask the Queen," Constance said, vowing to learn more about Lynara.

* * *

The fire burned furiously, flames crackling loudly, reaching for the stars. What was left of the army gathered around the pyre, their voices united in the Celtic death song. The mourners believed it helped the soul move from their world to the next. Boudicea made a small speech, keeping her praises simple, and then stood quietly beside Constance. When the historian asked her about Lynara's origin, the queen shook her head.

"She never said."

"And you never asked?"

"I didn't need to know her history. I trusted her. That was enough."

Constance shook her head. The logic eluded her. To trust someone you didn't know seemed foolish, especially for a queen. Still, if Boudicea didn't know where she came from, no one would.

"How long did you know her?"

Boudicea shrugged.

"About nine seasons. She came to me shortly after the Romans released me. Her skills as a warrior were superior to my other soldiers. I tried to make her a general, but she refused. She said she was a better warrior than officer. I had to order her to take a commission as a lieutenant."

Boudicea smiled, remembering the day she introduced her to the senior officers. Her generals had been shocked when she announced Lynara would be a general. When the young woman declined the commission, they were appalled she would refuse their queen.

Amused by their fickle attitude, Boudicea made Lynara a lieutenant. They were uncomfortable, but no one dared challenge their leader. In time, they realized Lynara was an exceptional warrior and grew to respect her skills in combat and battle strategies.

"Then I will write that down and everything else the others can tell me. Lynara will not be forgotten," Constance vowed.

"Do it well, historian. She deserves to be remembered for her sacrifice."

Boudicea patted her shoulder and walked away, her shoulders slumped and head bowed. The Queen felt the young woman's loss deeply.

* * *

Two weeks later, Constance received news that the Celtic queen was dead. The Romans had searched relentlessly for her, anxious to capture her so she could be paraded before Nero. Boudicea had stolen their thunder by committing suicide. It was a huge blow to the Roman ego and secured Boudicea's place forever in the histories of her people.

Hearing the news, Constance was saddened. The next day, she packed her scrolls and moved on. In time the memory of the historian amongst the Celts faded, as did that of her warrior.

CHAPTER 6

"SABBY, ARE you okay?" a voice asked, interrupting her thoughts. Raising her head, she was surprised to see Jennie standing in front of her. Normally, she could sense another's presence long before they arrived, but this particular memory always made her oblivious to events around her. For that reason alone, she did her best to avoid thinking of Constance. Unfortunately, her mind wouldn't release its grasp on the one woman she had truly loved. She would relive those moments over and over again for eternity.

Standing, she gave the young private a reassuring smile.

"I'm fine. Just daydreaming."

"From your expression, I'd say it was more of a nightmare," Jennie replied, giving her friend a closer look.

"I guess it depends on your perspective."

Slapping the woman on the shoulder, she gave her a light shove.

"Come on. We have work to do." Looking at the sun's position, she estimated she had another hour before the troops moved out.

"Yeah, I heard we were going out again. I hope this time turns out better than the last," she grumbled, remembering the three men who had been killed by landmines.

"You and me both, Jennie."

* * *

Two hours later, the squad climbed into three jeeps and headed toward the small village. They would drive to within two clicks and then travel the rest of the distance on foot. The drivers would return to base camp and await their pick-up call.

Approaching the village, the soldiers lay down on a ridge to check the activity. Several villagers milled around the open door of what was obviously a store. Baggy trousers, long shirts and a sash were the common dress of the local men. Skullcaps and turbans finished off their wardrobe. The women wore long dresses or skirts over their trousers and scarves on their heads.

"What do ya think, Sabby?"

"We'll wait here until dark. It's hard to tell which ones are insurgents and which are villagers."

"Or collaborators," Jennie said.

"Yeah. Send Willie and Samson to the other side of the hill to look around. Tell them to keep low. We don't want anyone knowing we're here yet."

"Gotcha."

Crawling off to give the two men their instructions, Jennie didn't notice the scorpion near her left hand until a knife sailed by and cut it in half.

"What the...Oh, thanks Sabby."

"Keep alert, Jennie. There are worse things than that out here."

"Sorry."

Sabnock nodded, grabbed the knife and then motioned her to move on. Turning back to watch the village, she noticed a group of men smoking cigarettes and huddling near a small house. One man kept looking at a particular ridge, his body language a clear indication he was nervous. Following the direction of his glances, the demoness spotted a well-traveled path. Obviously, the villager was expecting someone important. Pressing the throat mic against her neck, she called Samson.

"Samson, where you at?"

"About three hundred meters to your left, Sabby."

"Good. Back up a bit and watch that trail. I think we're going to have company very soon."

"Will do. Let me know if you see anything."

"Roger."

Sending two other soldiers in the opposite direction, she instructed them to concentrate on the men in the village, hoping they would give her more clues about the insurgents. When she noticed several villagers glancing nervously at some men standing by an open door, she was sure of their target.

"Squirrel. See if you can get someone on the radio that knows about this place. I want to know how many exits there are in that house and who lives there."

"Sure thing, Sabby."

Sabnock waited while he called to the base. She and Squirrel were the only ones who spoke Farsi. It was one of the reasons the locals trusted them and were willing to help them hunt for the militants who had invaded their homeland. The locals knew most of the foreigners pretending to be villagers weren't there to help them but to promote their own agenda of terror.

* * *

The sun settled below the horizon and the soldiers put on their night vision goggles. Everything turned an eerie green. Thirty minutes later, Sabnock spotted two men walking slowly down the path. Three others approached them and called out a greeting. After shaking hands, they talked for a few minutes and then all five turned around and disappeared back into the hills.

"Sabby, what do you think?" Samson asked over the communicator.

"I think they're going to get a surprise, but wait for my orders. We need to know everyone that's involved with this cell."

"Roger."

A short time later, eight men carrying four large crates staggered down the path toward the house. Sabnock instructed her men to let them enter the building before moving in.

"Okay, Squirrel, you and Chip take the east side and keep an eye out for anyone on the outside who may be watching. Samson, you and Willie take the south side. The rest of you keep an eye out for trouble from the villagers. Jennie and I will take the door. When I give the word, we all go in at once...and be careful."

Cautiously each team crept silently down the incline toward their target, making sure they weren't spotted. The sound of loud male voices came from several homes. Occasionally a woman's voice could be heard as she lectured someone to behave.

Once they were in position, Sabnock gave her final instructions, cautioning everyone to be careful and diligent. Then, giving the signal, eight soldiers burst through the windows and doors, leaving a half dozen outside to guard their backs. Surprised, some of the insurgents grabbed their rifles but were quickly killed. Sabnock did a quick body count and realized two men were missing.

"Shit! They're not all here."

"They have to be. No one left the house," Samson replied.

Hearing her troops yelling, she ran outside and saw several villagers with torches and rifles running toward them.

"Squirrel, get out here and tell them we're not after them."

Running past her, Squirrel waved his hands and yelled to the villagers to halt. As they slowed, he told them about the insurgents and that they weren't after anyone else. One man dressed in the typical garb of an Afghani approached Squirrel slowly, demanding an explanation. Hands flying wildly, it was obvious he wasn't happy and wanted to talk to person in charge.

"Sabby, you'd better get over here. This doesn't look good."

Turning to Jennie, she told her and the others to check out the rest of the house, especially the flooring, while she tried to calm things down. She had only walked about thirty paces when she heard a loud explosion and felt her body being tossed helplessly through the air. Landing painfully on her face, she twisted around to see the house in ruins, smoke and dust spreading through the air like a brown cloud. The sound of running feet distracted her momentarily from the carnage and she turned to shoot whoever the attacker was.

"Whoah, Sabby!" Squirrel yelled, holding his hands up defensively. Kneeling next to her, he checked for injuries.

"I'm fine," she hissed, although a sharp pain sliced through her back.

"I don't think so," he replied, pressing his hand against the five inch gash in her clothes. "You're bleeding pretty badly."

"I'm fine, I said. Go check the others."

Nodding, Squirrel realized it was useless to argue. Sabnock knew what she was doing. Running to the house, he and the other soldiers who had been standing guard on the perimeter searched the ruins for survivors.

"We've got three wounded and three dead!" he yelled.

"Get the helicopter here, ASAP!" The demoness yelled back and then grimaced as another pain tore through her. Sometimes, she wondered why she put herself though this type of thing, but knew it was the only thing that made her existence bearable.

It's getting pretty old, though, she thought. A hand touching her shoulder startled her. The villager Squirrel had been talking to was trying to get her attention.

"Amerkin, okay you?" he asked.

Sabnock nodded and motioned toward her men. Nodding his understanding, he signaled to the villagers to help the wounded. Samson, Willie and Chip were carried to a clearing for the helicopter. Jennie's body, along with the other two dead soldiers, was removed and covered with blankets provided by the women.

* * *

It took forty five minutes for the helicopters to arrive. The wounded and dead were loaded into one while fresh backups jumped out of the second. Sabnock refused to leave her remaining troops, knowing they still had to explain to the villagers what had happened. A medic put a compression bandage on her wound.

"You better get that taken care of when you get back to base. There's some nasty shit you can catch if you're not careful."

"Thanks, Crappy. I'll be fine."

"Yeah, yeah. Well, let me put it another way. If you don't get it taken care of, I'll put you on report."

"Okay! Can't you go bug someone else?"

Snickering, the medic walked away. He loved picking on the infamous Corporal Sabnock, especially knowing he could irritate her so well.

* * *

Two hours later, jeeps arrived to take the remaining soldiers back to base. After Sabnock explained to the Afghani leader about the insurgents, the weapons and explosives stashed in the house, the villagers returned to their homes satisfied they hadn't been attacked.

As they prepared for the return trip to camp no one spoke. Each knew it could have been any one of them in those body bags. Losing members from their squadron was painful.

"You going to get looked at, Sabby?" Squirrel asked.

"I want to check on the guys first. Then I'll get patched up."

"I just don't understand any of this. All this hatred and killing. Why are we even here? It's not like we're going to solve anything."

"Probably not, but humans having been fighting useless wars for a long time. It's their nature."

Squirrel picked up a stone and angrily flung it at a nearby Hummer.

"Yeah, I guess, but this..." he said, sweeping his arms out to indicate the land around them. "This land isn't worth dying for."

"Maybe not to you, but apparently it is to the locals and some political groups."

"Well, I don't want to die here defending people who won't even stand up for themselves. Hell, while I'm sitting here talking to you, someone could put a bullet through my head."

Sabnock looked at the young man but refused to look into his future. She didn't want to know when Death would call on him. Looking off into the distance, she grimaced.

"I know what you mean. Death is like an assassin or sniper hiding in the darkness and shadows. It sees Its target and patiently waits for the right moment to take the shot — and we never know when that will be."

"Yeah!" Squirrel sighed, tossing another stone at the vehicle. "Aren't you even a little bit afraid you might be the next target?"

Sabnock shrugged, knowing permanent death wasn't an option for her.

"It's not something I think about. What's the use? No one knows when Death will come. The best we can do is live each moment as if it were our last and hope this life is enough. Only after we are dead will we know the truth."

"Truth?"

"Never mind, Squirrel. Now isn't the time for philosophy. I need to call Jennie's mom. I hate this part. How do I tell her that her daughter is dead when I promised to take care of her?"

"It wasn't your fault," Squirrel said quietly, knowing his leader always took their losses hard.

Sabnock gave him an odd look and walked away.

If only you knew, she thought. Sabnock could have prevented the fatal outcome if she had used her powers to find the missing insurgents. It would have been so easy to discover their hiding place. That was the dilemma. The demoness knew her men depended on her to guide them and make the right decisions.

Without using her powers, she tried to keep that trust, knowing it was the only way to keep from seriously altering future events. She was not willing to do that although she knew everything she did had its own effect on the future. Sabnock believed that her actions as a human caused only minor changes – if even that. After all, there were many soldiers capable of doing her job almost as well.

CHAPTER 7

THE BODIES OF the dead soldiers were shipped back to the states two days later. The other three were transported to a hospital in Bitburg, Germany. They had sustained serious injuries, but would survive. Unfortunately, two would be severely crippled.

Sabnock's injury took twenty-three stitches after a small piece of shrapnel was removed. The angle of its entry had left a large gash across her right shoulder blade. Although painful, the demoness considered it more a nuisance than anything else. She had wanted to remain with the rest of her unit but received new orders to report back to the States after taking time off for her injury. Because she had accumulated leave time, Sabnock decided to combine her medical leave with her time off and take a trip.

"Got any idea where you'll be stationed next, Sabby?" Squirrel asked. She had told her unit about her orders. No one was happy about it. Many believed her calm approach to tough situations had saved them from serious injuries or even death.

"Yeah, Fort Benning in Georgia."

"Bugs are horrible there. They have roaches as big as skateboards."

Squirrel shuddered thinking of the two years of hell he had spent there. Hot summers, mosquitoes, no-see-ums...and just about every type of snake you could think of. He *hated* creepy crawlies and biting bugs.

"So I've heard."

"At least you'll have a few weeks of leave before you have to report. What are you going to do with yourself?"

"Travel. I've had an urge to visit the Carpathian Mountains. Maybe do a little sightseeing around Transylvania."

"Geez, Sabby. I hear they have werewolves and vampires in that place. You think that's a good idea?"

Sabnock laughed. If Squirrel knew the truth about her, he'd realize that those creatures weren't much of a threat to a demoness.

"Don't worry," she replied. "I'll make sure I carry a wooden stake or two."

"And a cross. Don't forget that!"

Realizing Squirrel was serious, she sobered slightly. He had good reason to fear the unknown.

"Alright, I'll pick some up," she promised, wanting to alleviate his worries.

* * *

Two days later she was packed and on her way to Moldova and the Carpathian Mountains. She had told Squirrel she had an urge to visit the place but in reality it had been an almost overwhelming compulsion. Something demanded her presence.

Normally, she would use the available military transports. Those could take several days, though, and for some reason she felt it was imperative to get there as quickly as possible. Sabnock caught a red-eye special to Cahul and then rented a car and raced toward the town of Teraclia. It was essential that she arrive in time. The question was, in time for what?

After checking into a hotel, the demoness spent several hours walking around the downtown area, trying to discover what had drawn her to the town. Finding nothing, she stopped at a restaurant and ate a light meal before heading back to her room.

It was then that she spotted the old woman shuffling down the sidewalk, her body pressing slightly forward against the cold gusts of wind blowing from the nearby mountains. Only her determination gave her the strength to win the battle.

Gray-haired, slightly stooped and frail looking, it was obvious her health was failing, but it made her no less beautiful. She *felt* familiar to the demoness.

Sabnock leaned against the building, unconsciously flicking a cigarette lighter on and off as she thought about her next move. The small lighter fascinated her. She could stare into its flames and see the fires of home, a small comfort for someone who refused to return to the land of her origin.

"It can't be her," the demoness reasoned. "She would have to be over two-thousand human years old."

That argument alone should have settled the issue. Still, Sabnock shook her head. Her demon senses knew the truth.

Two people passing by looked at her nervously. The demoness gave them an evil grin and they scurried off.

Chuckling, she pushed away from the wall and walked across the street. Entering the building, she saw the woman talking with the hotel clerk. Sabnock waited at the entrance for the woman to turn around, curious to see if she would be recognized.

* * *

Constance was tired. Actually, she was beyond tired. The centuries had taken their toll and her days were numbered, which was why she had returned to Teraclia. The manuscripts of her people and her life needed to be given to Dakota. The young journalist was the perfect guardian for them, even though she didn't have long to live by the historian's standards. Constance's people, the Gebians, were long lived. Human life spans were short but nonetheless just as important in the greater scheme of life.

Turning away from the clerk, she leaned heavily on her cane. The elevator seemed so far. The next thing she knew, her elbow was being gently grasped, helping to support her while she gathered her strength.

"Thank you, young woman," she gasped, trying to catch her breath.

"My pleasure, ma'am," Sabnock replied, not sure what to do.

The two women moved slowly to the elevator. Constance leaned heavily on the arm that was helping her. Once inside, she pushed the second floor button and then sighed.

"Getting old can be hell," she quipped, glancing up at the face of the woman in uniform. The light in the elevator was behind the tall figure, shading her face.

"I can only imagine."

Chuckling, Constance patted the hand holding her arm.

"All in good time, deary."

Sabnock didn't know what to say so she remained quiet. The opening of the door prevented any further conversation.

"I can make it from here. Thank you for your help," Constance said, her breathing less labored.

"I've come this far, ma'am, a few more feet won't hurt."

Secretly the historian was relieved. Even short distances were difficult for her, and there was something comforting about the young woman's presence. It had been a long time since she had experienced that feeling.

Reaching the hotel room door, she fished in her handbag for her key. She tried to insert it in the slot but her hand shook badly. Gently, the stranger took the key from her fingers and unlocked the door.

Pushing it open, Sabnock helped Constance into the room and removed her worn overcoat. Folding it neatly, she placed it on the table and then pulled out the chair for the old woman to sit.

"Have you eaten?"

The historian looked up at the woman and again found her face hidden by the shadows.

"No. I rarely feel hungry at my age," she replied, squinting at the light shining in her eyes. "Sit, please."

Waving her toward the other chair, she leaned back and watched as the soldier moved gracefully away and sat.

Crossing her long legs, Sabnock reached up and removed her cap, placing it on her lap. Constance frowned when she saw the short, red hair.

"What's your name, young woman?"

"Sabnock, ma'am."

"Well, Sabnock, stop with the ma'am. I feel old enough already without having to listen to that word."

"Yes ma'am," the demoness replied and smiled, knowing it would aggravate the historian.

"You young people show no respect nowadays," Constance responded grumpily.

"No, ma'am. What would you like me to call you?"

"Constance, and don't you dare call me Connie. I detest that name."

Even though Sabnock had known this was her Constance, it still shocked her when it was confirmed.

"Well, Miss Constance, I..."

"Cut out the Miss too. I'm plain, ordinary Constance."

"Okay, well, plain, ordinary Constance, since you haven't eaten and neither have I, perhaps you would allow me to buy you dinner. I'm sure the hotel has room service."

"Now why would you want to do that?"

"You remind me of someone I knew a long time ago, and I'm hungry."

The historian laughed.

"My dear, you can't be more than thirty, so it can't be that long ago."

"Time is sometimes irrelevant, don't you think?" Sabnock asked.

Constance leaned forward in her chair to get a better look at her young companion. There was definitely something familiar about her.

"Do I know you?"

"Have you been to Afghanistan recently?"

"No. I was there a long time ago, but long before you were born, child."

"Then I'd have to say not in this life," Sabnock replied, making a joke out of what she knew was the truth. "So, can I buy dinner?"

"Why not?" Constance said, not wanting to be alone. She would soon be more alone than at any other time in her life. Tonight, accepting this woman's company felt right.

"Good. Let me guess, you like steak, extremely rare or a beef or lamb stew."

"You're quite intuitive, but I can't eat something that heavy anymore. It doesn't sit well on the stomach."

"Okay, how about some French Onion soup and fresh bread."

Nodding, Constance leaned back in her chair and closed her eyes. Something about the young soldier seemed very familiar. Her voice, her red hair and her demeanor made her think of her warrior, but she knew it wasn't possible. Fate was just being cruel to remind her of the one person she had truly loved.

Sabnock called room service and ordered their meals. Then she waited patiently for the historian to say something. When she didn't, the demoness grew worried. It was obvious Constance had only a short time left in this life. Although saddened, Sabnock also felt hope, knowing she could search for her in the Underworld. Contrary to human belief, it wasn't just a place for the condemned, but also a place for the flawed...and most humans were flawed. Few were able to lead the exemplary life that permitted their passage into the Twin's realm.

Everyone knew Dis' sibling ran an orderly realm and hated any sort of disruption. Those that fit best in the Overworld were the gentle and passive, or those willing to sacrifice their existence and lives trying to help the needy.

His world was a place filled with eclectic souls contented to quietly go about their business being creative and unnoticed.

Of course, the Twin also allowed the real heroes entry for he needed to keep his legions filled with souls brave enough to defend the realm. It kept the Underworld and Overworld armies balanced. Sabnock knew that balance was a necessity in all things.

As for Constance, from the short time they had spent together long ago, Sabnock knew she was no angel. Filled with fire and passion, the historian enjoyed life and had the appetite for all that it could offer. The demoness was confused about how Constance could still be alive. Humans were lucky if they made it to a hundred.

"Are you okay?" she asked, her acute hearing picking up the slowed heartbeat.

"I'm just a little tired."

A knock interrupted them. Sabnock opened the door and took the tray from the hotel attendant. Handing him his money, she shouldered the door shut and put the tray on the table. Placing the soup and a glass of water near Constance, she grabbed her own bowl and sat down. Both women ate in silence.

"Ah, that was good," the historian said, pushing her bowl aside.

"Yes. It's certainly better than Army chow."

"I can imagine. How long have you been a soldier?"

"All my life."

"A born soldier, huh?" the historian teased.

"You might say that. What do you do?"

"Me? I'm an historian."

"Do you teach?"

"No, I record history. At least I used to. I'm too old and tired for that now."

"Have you always been an historian?"

"All my life."

"A born historian," Sabnock said, unable to resist teasing her.

Constance chuckled.

"Enough about me. What brings you to Teraclia? You're obviously an American and this place isn't exactly a tourist trap."

"Curiosity. I had some leave coming and decided to check out the land of vampires and werewolves. I've always been curious about the dark side of humanity."

"I certainly understand that. Imagination can be a great thing, but it brings with it its own demons."

Sabnock couldn't help but laugh at the irony of the comment.

"I suppose so," she agreed, smiling. "I take it you don't believe in those things."

"Oh, I believe alright. I've seen many things in my life and would have to say those would be some of the least strange."

"Now that sounds rather ominous."

Constance leaned forward to get a better look at her guest.

"You look like you don't scare easily," she commented and then shifted the table lamp to improve the lighting. Frowning, she rubbed her tired eyes and tried again to focus on the woman's face.

Everything seems so blurry tonight, she thought.

"Maybe I should go now," Sabnock offered.

"No, no. It's just that you remind me of someone I knew long ago."

95

"Someone important?"

"Yes. Very."

"Would you tell me about her?"

"You don't want to waste your time listening to an old woman rambling," Constance replied, patting Sabnock's hand. "Don't you have someone to meet? A handsome woman like you can't be here alone."

"I'm pretty much a loner. There's no one, and I really want to know about her, if you don't mind. You loved her, didn't you?"

The historian hesitated, not sure if she wanted to expose her deepest feelings to a stranger. Still, the short time she had with her warrior was the happiest in her life and she wanted someone to know, really know, how special Lynara was. Maybe talking about her would give her short existence more meaning.

"She was a warrior, like you," the historian began.

"Warrior. It's a word not very often used anymore."

"Yes, but it's the appropriate word for her. Lynara was a lieutenant, young and handsome. You remind me of her. Her hair was red, like yours, but long and flowing. No matter, to me she was more than just handsome. She was brave, honest and true to herself."

"She sounds almost too perfect," Sabnock teased.

"No, she wasn't perfect, but she was good. I've never met anyone like her since."

"Good? How?"

Constance shrugged.

"It's hard to explain."

"What happened to her?"

"She died! She could have stayed with me and lived. I believe she would have if I had only asked her to. Our love was strong."

"But you didn't ask her."

"No. I think it would have killed our love. She was a warrior first. Duty, to her, was the most important thing."

"Are you so sure?" Sabnock asked, remembering back to when she had chosen to live, but too late.

"Yes. Besides, there were other factors that would have made staying together impossible."

"If you really loved each other, nothing should have stopped you."

"You are young and idealistic. There are some things that are insurmountable, even with love."

"Like what?"

"Death."

"You don't believe in an afterlife?"

"Well, yes."

"Then there's hope."

Constance chuckled.

"Where were you when I was a lot younger?"

The question gave Sabnock the opening she needed, but she wasn't sure if she wanted to take it. Would it really serve any purpose to let Constance know who she really was? Then again, was there any harm in letting her know the truth?

"Now don't go taking me so seriously, young woman. I'm way too old to jump your bones."

"Oh, I think you still have it in you," Sabnock teased, "and I consider it a compliment that you still want to."

Constance was about to comment when she caught the word *still*.

Just a figure of speech, she thought, *and the wishful thinking of an old woman.*

"I have to say, you do remind me so much of her, Sabnock. That is such an unusual name. I don't think I've ever met anyone with it, although I know it has a meaning. I just can't remember now."

"I doubt if you'll find many people who want to name their children that. Sabnock was a female demon. She commanded the legions of Satan. At least, that's what the legends say."

"And your parents named you after her? Were they devil worshippers?"

Sabnock grinned.

"No. Actually, I never knew my parents. As for the name, well, I'm not sure how I came about it."

"Well, someone had to give it to you. Children don't just choose their own names. Maybe you were a rambunctious child and your foster parents started calling you that."

"I never had parents of any kind. I pretty much have been on my own all my life."

"How sad! Everyone should have someone to love."

"Constance, do you mind if I ask you a personal question?"

"You can ask. It doesn't mean I'll answer."

Sabnock smirked.

"If you could live those moments over again...with Lynara...would you choose differently?"

"Knowing what I know now? I'm not sure. I'd like to think I would be brave enough to let her go. Then again, I think we could have made it work. Maybe I should have let her make the choice. Those two weeks, well, I'm being selfish now, but I would have sold my soul to have her with me for as long as possible if I thought I could make her happy."

"Then why didn't you call out to her?"

"I almost did. I wanted to. I..." Constance stopped. *Call out to her?* How did she know? Shaking her head, the historian hesitated. "How did you know?"

Sabnock stood and then knelt in front of her. Taking the withered hands in her own, she began running her thumbs across the palms.

"You still don't recognize me, do you?" she asked softly.

Constance gently disengaged one hand, touched the demoness' cheek and then her red hair. Green eyes stared unblinkingly back at her.

"Lynara?"

Sabnock nodded and pressed her lover's hand firmly against her cheek.

"But, you're dead! We burned your body."

"Yes, and you're still alive. I think we both have a lot of explaining to do."

"I should say so. You can't be a reincarnation. I've always thought it possible but never really believed in it."

"No, I'm not reincarnated. Listen, I think you should get some rest. We can talk about this tomorrow."

As much as she hated postponing the discussion until later, Constance had to agree. Already, she felt sluggish and unable to think clearly.

"Maybe that's a good idea. Where are you staying?"

Sabnock knew their time together was short. Although she didn't know the exact hour of her lover's death, she didn't want to chance it happening while she was away.

"I have a hotel room a few blocks away but if you don't mind, I'd like to stay here. We've been apart too long."

"You aren't thinking of taking advantage of an old woman?" Constance teased.

"No, but that doesn't mean I'm not thinking of taking advantage of you," Sabnock bantered back. "Now, let's get you ready for bed."

"And just where are you going to sleep, young woman?"

"I'm a soldier, remember? I can fall asleep just about anywhere, so these chairs will be fine."

"You'll do no such thing. I can't rest knowing you're sitting over there in that thing trying to sleep. This bed is big enough for the both of us."

"And you accused me of wanting to take advantage of you?" Sabnock teased.

"Pffft! As if."

"That's too bad. I was looking forward to it."

"Me too. Later, when I've regained some of my energy," the historian said, feeling almost young again. She knew it was an illusion, but enjoyed imagining it would happen. "Let's get some rest."

Helping Constance into bed, Sabnock pulled the quilt up and then lay down beside her. Closing her eyes, she pretended to sleep. Her lover fell asleep instantly. Sabnock waited patiently, making sure Constance was warm and comfortable.

Four hours later, she got up, picked up the phone and ordered a light meal for the two of them, knowing it was only a matter of a few minutes before the historian would wake up. When she stirred, her warrior helped her get into the chair. Walking to the door, Sabnock opened it as the waiter was about to knock. Taking the platter, she paid the bill and then closed the door.

"I've never had anyone wait on me like this. It's rather nice."

"I would have done this every day of your life, if I hadn't taken so long to make up my mind," Sabnock said.

"Make up your mind?"

"About us. I wanted to stay with you. I had decided to but Death stopped me."

"I know," Constance said.

"No, Constance, you don't know. What I'm trying to say is I..." *How do I explain this so it doesn't make her think I'm crazy or give her a heart attack?* "I'm not what you think."

"I don't understand," Constance said, confused.

"I know. This is difficult. When we fell in love, you thought I was human. I'm not! I'm a demon."

The silence was so loud both women wondered why they weren't deafened by it.

"That's pretty incredible."

"Incredible like unbelievable or incredible like you believe me?"

"Sabn...Lynara, you've never lied to me and you're here now. How can I not believe you?"

"How could you not?" Lynara chided gently. "Speaking of being here, you have some explaining to do as well."

"I guess you're not the only one with secrets."

"Apparently not. It looks like you've been keeping one for over two-thousand years."

"More like seven."

"Seven?"

Lynara was stunned. No human could live that long. "Are you human?" she asked.

"Yes and no, I'm not a demon, I'm a Gebian. We're long-lived."

"So it seems. Why haven't I ever heard of Gebians?"

"We tend to keep to ourselves. It would create *issues* if humans knew about us. It *is* strange though that you didn't know about us."

"Maybe not. I really wasn't interested in humanity in the beginning. We demons were too busy fighting another war. As for the humans, they certainly would want to study you. They've been searching for my kind for a long time. If they ever proved we were real, it would create havoc."

"Considering their opinions of demons, now, I'd say that's putting it mildly."

The two fell into a comfortable silence thinking of things that might have been had they been more honest with each other. Constance finally spoke.

"You said you changed your mind."

"Yes. I was torn between my vow to live and die as a human or spend what little time we would have together. Had I known it could have lasted this long, the choice would have been simple."

"I doubt it," Constance said, although she knew she would have chosen Lynara over two-thousand years of loneliness. "Choices are never that easy, especially when it comes to love and being true to yourself."

"I would have chosen you," Lynara said firmly. The historian didn't doubt her.

Constance sighed. So many years alone, wasted, because neither had spoken what was in her heart, and now it was too late.

"And I would have chosen you. It seems we both had a lapse in judgment," she said and then laughed. "Just my luck to find out at the end of my life."

"This life."

Before Constance could respond, she felt a sharp pain shoot across her chest and down her arm. Gasping, she bent forward and pressed her hand against her abdomen just below her breasts. Seeing her distress, Lynara stood and picked up the frail woman and placed her gently on the bed. Both knew the end was near.

"Lynara..." she gasped, barely able to catch her breath. "You must...do something...for me."

"Anything."

Constance pointed to a set of manuscripts on a small stand in the corner.

"You must take...take them to Dakota Dev...Devereaux."

"What are they?"

"The his...history of my...people."

"Okay. Where will I find her?"

The historian's breathing became more labored.

"Add...ress inside."

"I'll take care of it. You just rest now."

Lying next to her lover, Lynara gathered the slender body in her arms and held her tight. She could feel the life force slowly slipping away.

"I'll be...doing that s...soon enough. I wish we...had...more time together."

"I could give it to you," Lynara offered. "I could make you well."

As a demon, she had the ability to extend mortal lives. Other demons used the power to manipulate mortals into doing what they wanted.

Shaking her head, Constance knew this wasn't like before. It was one thing for the demoness to choose life. To her, dying wasn't real. For the historian, it was a natural progression even if she was long lived. Changing her destiny wouldn't just impact her but would alter the future for a lot of people. It wasn't something she was willing to do, even if it meant sacrificing her and Lynara's happiness.

"The price...too high."

"It's a risk I'm willing to take if it gives us a little more time."

"But I'm not. This isn't...just about us." Constance took a few quick breaths. "It's about what's...right. What...we decide...to...tonight affects more than just us." Again she hesitated, inhaling deeply. "It's my time...I will ful...fill my destiny."

"So we do this again," Lynara said sadly.

Constance laughed and then started coughing, her body racked with spasms. Although forbidden to interfere with the death process, the demoness decided there was no reason for her lover to suffer unnecessarily. The pain and shortness of breath subsided.

"You didn't do anything..."

"No, I didn't heal you. I would never go against your wishes."

"Thank you."

They lay quietly together for a few minutes until Lynara remembered the manuscripts.

"Tell me about your people."

Constance chuckled.

"It would take a lifetime."

"Then tell me about the manuscripts. That's why you came here isn't it? To give them to this Devereaux? Why her?"

"I trust her to protect them. To protect the secret of my people."

"Is she one of you?"

104

"No. She's human, but she's special."

"What will happen to those records when she dies? Humans have such short lives."

"I don't know. I'm hoping she'll find someone to give them to. It'll be out of my control by then."

Lynara knew Constance was worried about the papers and her people's future. If the manuscripts fell into the wrong hands, it would be disastrous for the Gebians.

"I can take them if she doesn't," the demoness offered.

"And what would you do with them?" Constance teased. "They wouldn't last very long where you're from."

"Yeah, I can see where that might be a problem. I promise not to take them to the Underworld, although you'd be surprised at the technology we have there. Some of us even have ice for our drinks."

"Ice! In Hell! I don't believe it."

"Like I said. We're quite advanced."

They both laughed thinking of the old adage about snowballs in hell.

"Seriously. I *will* make sure they're protected. Your people will be safe."

"I appreciate that. Thank you."

Relieved, Constance relaxed into Sabnock's warm embrace. Although the pain was gone, she felt the cold fingers of death closing in on her. Shivering, she tried to burrow deeper in her lover's arms, remembering the heat and passion of long ago.

Lynara knew Death intimately. She understood It's cold touch. Raising her core heat, she increased her skin temperature several degrees.

"Is that better?" she asked.

"Yes, much. Your arms are so warm. Do you still have those tattoos?" The shivering stopped.

"They are a part of me. Dis, himself, bestowed them upon me. Only two others bear the royal symbol of my Lord."

"He still holds your allegiance?" Constance sounded surprised, stiffening slightly.

"He has my respect and my loyalty. He isn't my master now. I owe my allegiance to no one...but you."

"I'm glad. No one should own another."

"Dis has never owned me, Constance. I pledged myself freely to him. He has never forced any of his Legion to follow him."

"Not the devil I've heard about then," she said, the historian in her rising to the surface.

"He never was what mortals thought. Dis is Dis. Arrogant...self-centered...imperfect...but always fair to those who serve him."

Constance shifted to a more comfortable position and relaxed, relishing the warmth of Lynara's embrace.

"Lynara?"

"What, my love?"

"What happens to my soul when I die?"

"I'm not sure. I think you'll go to the Underworld. Most souls go there."

Constance laughed.

"I've done a lot of things I regret, but I didn't think I was that bad."

The demoness chuckled and gave her a gentle hug. Constance was unaware that the tattoos were searing her arms and legs, leaving identical impressions on her withered skin. Lynara was making sure that all others in the Underworld knew Constance was hers.

"It's not about being bad, at least for some. It's just that the Overworld usually takes only those that have led exemplary lives or humans who made great sacrifices."

"That leaves me out."

A sudden tiredness overwhelmed Constance. Feeling lethargic, she knew her time had come and closed her eyes. Lynara waited, knowing she could do nothing more to ease her lover's passage into Death's hands.

Placing her cheek against the silver hair, she began to rock her back and forth, humming a soothing song from her own world. She made sure to keep her body heat high enough to keep Constance warm.

"It's okay, my love," she whispered. "I'm here with you."

"Lynara? Will you join me after I'm dead?"

"As if you needed to ask. We'll finally have a life together."

"Longer than the last two," Constance said and smiled.

"Longer than the last two," Lynara agreed. "An eternity."

Constance sighed. Death had arrived. Normally impatient, It recognized the demoness and hesitated.

"What would you have me do?" It asked, giving Sabnock a choice.

Looking at her lover, Lynara felt the tears streaming down her cheeks and hugged the frail body tenderly.

"What you must. She welcomes your arrival."

"So be it."

The historian's heart beat became slower and slower. Constance felt her life force slipping away. Taking her final breath, she struggled to speak.

"Thank...you...for finding...me," she gasped. "I... love...you. I...will al...ways love..."

"You," Lynara said, finishing the sentence. "Don't be afraid, my love. I'll be there to catch you."

CHAPTER 8

THE UNDERWORLD was just as magnificent as when Sabnock had last seen it, perhaps more so since it had grown over the millennia. Walking to the Tower of Souls, she attracted several strange glances. It had been thousands of years since the warrior demoness had appeared on the streets of their realm. Something important was up and the minions wondered if Dis was planning some sort of attack on his Twin. They hoped not. It would mean fighting another great war and no one was eager to go through that again.

Pushing the huge doors open, she walked up to Soulkeeper.

"I'm here to retrieve a soul," she stated, giving him no option for debate.

"Certainly, Sabnock. It's good to see you again. It's been a long time. What soul are you looking for this time?"

"Constance Loh Rehn. She just arrived."

"Loh Rehn? Haven't you found her yet?"

Soulkeeper never forgot a name and Sabnock had returned many times before looking for this particular soul. One day the demoness stopped returning to the keeper's vault. Soulkeeper assumed she had finally found who she was looking for. Apparently she hadn't.

"I wouldn't be here if I had," growled Sabnock.

Signaling for a small minion to approach, Soulkeeper ordered it to find the soul and bring it to them. Scurrying off, it disappeared into another room. Minutes later, it came scrambling back, wringing its hands nervously.

"No soul, master," it squeaked.

"What do you mean, no soul, you moron? Of course she's here," Soulkeeper yelled. "Sabnock says she is. Now, go back and look again."

"Yes, Master. I go," the minion cried, not wanting to anger its owner.

"It's hard to find good help nowadays," Soulkeeper grumbled, shaking his head.

Minutes later the minion crept back, trembling. "I no find," it sobbed, tears streaming down its cheeks.

"What's the problem?" Sabnock demanded.

"Umm, Rastis can't find Loh Rehn. Are you sure she's dead?"

"Would I be here if she wasn't?"

"Well, ummm..." the Soulkeeper shrugged, not wanting to remind the demoness of her previous inquiries – two-hundred-forty-three to be exact.

"Where else could she be? This is where mortal souls come."

"I know. Maybe she's gone to the Overworld. Some do manage to meet the Twin's requirements. Was she that type?"

"No, she belongs here. Is it possible someone captured her soul before it got here?"

"Only if she was scheduled for punishment. Then she'd go directly to the assigned demon. Let me check the records."

Pulling out a large, brown book, Soulkeeper flipped through the pages.

"She's not listed anywhere in the Necronomicon. At the moment, all of the demons have received their latest assignments and there's no Loh Rehn."

"I didn't realize you still used that thing to keep track of the demons and their charges," Sabnock said, studying the yellowed pages. "You don't have computers down here?"

Soulkeeper snickered.

"I wouldn't have one of those things in here if Dis ordered me to. They're way too unreliable. Besides, I heard they carry viruses."

The demoness shook her head. Soulkeeper was one of those demons who preferred to live in the past. In a way, though, Sabnock found it comforting. The old ways weren't all bad.

"Could she have done something to attract the attention of the Tribunal?"

"No. She wasn't evil."

"Hmmm. I wonder..." Soulkeeper hesitated.

"What?" Sabnock growled impatiently.

"Well, Dis might have taken her. He has rights to every soul, but it would be highly unusual to do so without my knowledge."

"Not if he wanted me back!" Sabnock said angrily and stormed off.

"This isn't good." Soulkeeper mumbled, looking at the little minion hiding behind a small statue.

111

"No good, master, no good," it echoed, bobbing its head up and down.

* * *

Dis was enjoying a few minutes of peace away from his guests. There were moments when even he grew weary of the orgies. Coke in hand, he stood on the balcony looking at the ever-present fires burning throughout the realm. Orange and red flames danced seductively as they flared high into the blue and silver sky. The contrasting colors made the Underworld feel wild and vibrant. He reveled in its beauty and the fact that all of it belonged to him.

Returning to his chamber, he settled in his recliner, closed his eyes and thought about the Child. In time, she was going to cause him a great deal of trouble. She was ambitious and powerful, a potent combination. He would have to make sure his spies kept a close watch on her. It was going to be interesting from now on.

A loud disturbance in the next room caught his attention. Three minions came scurrying in, highly agitated, followed by a tall demoness, one he hadn't seen in a very long time.

"Sabnock!" he bellowed, surprised at her bravado.

"Lord Dis," she acknowledged, an old habit too deeply ingrained to forget.

"You didn't announce yourself. Have you forgotten your place?"

"No, I haven't, but perhaps you've forgotten I no longer serve you."

"All demons serve me at my leisure, Sabnock. Releasing you from your obligations may give you some sense of freedom, but don't think it grants you immunity against my wrath, or from conscripting you back into my Legion."

"I'm no longer yours to command or threaten, Dis. You may ask me to serve you, and I will do so if the cause is just, but I won't be ordered by you or intimidated by your threats."

"You've grown impudent during your absence. Freedom has spoiled you, but I'll overlook it since you served me well in the past. Don't take it for a weakness, though. Now, what do you want?"

"I'm looking for a soul. Soulkeeper doesn't have her and neither do any of the torturers. You're the only other one capable of retrieving her."

Throwing back his head, Dis laughed so hard it almost hurt. To think that one of his demons dared to intrude on his privacy, and then have the nerve to want what was his, was priceless.

"I have many souls, but what makes you think I would release one of them to you?" he asked and then motioned to his minions to leave them. "Sit, Sabnock. Fortunately for you, you have piqued my curiosity. Whose soul is so valuable you would chance my anger to retrieve it?"

"Her name is Constance Loh Rehn."

"A human? You disturb my peace for a human?"

"No. She calls her people Gebians."

"Ah, them! Worshippers of Isis and Geb."

"You know of them?"

"Of course. They were minor gods," Dis replied, waving his hand dismissively. "They passed a long time ago."

"Passed? Passed where?"

Dis shrugged.

"Who knows? The same place the others went, I suppose. They were never a threat to me so I had no reason to think about them."

"Like the other gods and goddesses who were."

"They disrupted my plans. Don't tell me you've grown a conscience after all this time?"

"I could care less about them. All I want is the soul."

Snapping his fingers, Dis leaned back in his chair. A small deformed minion with tiny horns and dark red skin scurried in, its hooves clicking on the polished floors.

"Grasrak, do we have the soul of a Constance Loh Rehn?"

"No, master. We no have souls now."

"None?" Dis asked, surprised. "Why not?"

"You no choose now. No interest, you say."

"What about the ones we had?"

"All gone...all gone."

"Gone where?"

"Brimstone Abyss," the minion replied, nervously.

"Hmmm. I must be getting a little absent-minded." Dis said, stroking his chin. "Oh well, it's not like there's a shortage. You can go now, Grasrak." The minion disappeared as quickly as he came. "Looks like you're going to have to look elsewhere. She's definitely not here."

Sabnock had no choice but to accept his word. Dis was many things, but he would never lie to her. Power was a strong incentive to keep his demons and minions in check, but the Underlord knew the wisdom of keeping them loyal. Lying to them would compromise his authority and ultimately make his job as ruler harder.

"Where else could she be?" she wondered out loud, frustrated.

"Not with my Twin. He would never accept anyone from that race. They would be too deviant for his taste," Dis offered. "Why is this soul so important to you? There are plenty here to choose from."

"That's not your concern," Sabnock snapped.

"Careful, demoness," he warned, his body stiffening angrily. "There's a limit to my patience and my generosity. You come here wanting something that would be mine and then behave in this manner?"

The demoness realized she was pushing her luck. It was true she took her freedom seriously, but she knew that Dis was very capable of imprisoning her if he decided to. Besides, he was right. All souls in the Underworld were his.

"You're right. I apologize, My Lord."

Nodding, Dis relaxed.

"Good. You haven't forgotten your place."

Sabnock was about to object when he held up his hand.

"Enough. Arguing serves no purpose. I don't have the soul and I know my Twin doesn't. I suggest you look elsewhere, maybe where the lesser gods disappeared to."

"And where is that? You've already said you don't know where they went."

"I don't, but I can think of a good possibility. It's the one place that makes sense — The Great Beyond."

"I thought that was just a concept, something to explain the mystery behind the disappearance of angels and demons."

"It's real, but not easily found. Even I'm not sure where to begin."

"Someone must know."

Feeling her frustration, Dis frowned.

"This soul, it's that important?"

"More than life itself," Sabnock vowed, her voice reflecting a longing he understood, although would never reveal that fact.

"You love this Gebian?"

The demoness looked into the chocolate-brown eyes, expecting to see amusement. Instead, she saw curiosity and maybe something more.

"Yes."

Remembering back to a time when the human Lilith had been his wife, Dis nodded his understanding. Even after all this time, she still had a special place in his heart, but it was a weakness he never dared reveal.

"There may be a way, but I can't promise anything."

"I'll be in your debt if you can help me," Sabnock said reluctantly, knowing what he could demand.

"Be careful, Sabnock. I may collect that debt."

"I wouldn't say it if I didn't mean it," she replied stiffly.

"You must love her a great deal. Now go. Grasrak will let you know if I find out anything."

Knowing there was nothing else she could do, Sabnock left.

Maybe I should have said thank you, she thought.

Not even a thank you, Dis thought and then laughed. *A good thing, too. I'd hate to think one of my best commanders has grown weak from love. Now I wonder where I can find the Traveler. I'm surprised she hasn't popped in uninvited by now. That's definitely a female trait. Most undesirable.*

CHAPTER 9

SABNOCK RETURNED to the hotel room to tend to the physical needs of her lover. Not knowing if Constance had made any arrangements for her remains, she searched the documents and manuscripts for any clues that could help her. Every now and then she would look longingly at the woman lying on the bed.

"I could have saved you," she murmured. "We could have had a life if you had let me. Where are you now? Why can't I find you?"

They were questions with no answers. If Dis couldn't help her, she wasn't sure what she would do, but she would never give up the search. She had promised Constance they would be together and Sabnock kept her promises, even if it took an eternity.

Picking up the manuscripts, she glanced through them, stopping every now and then to read something that caught her eye. When she came across the time period they had met, she saw her name and was curious how the historian would describe their moments together. It was like living every minute over again.

The detailed conversations were almost word for word. Her skills at remembering were extraordinary and her ability to describe events precise. That alone impressed the demoness, but what brought hot tears to her eyes was the description of their lovemaking. Every word, every phrase was woven together like threads in a tapestry. When the picture was complete, anyone reading the story would feel the heat and the passion of their love.

The demoness ran her fingertips gently over the words as if by touching them she would relive the moments. Slowly closing the manuscript, she placed it on the table, walked over to the body and lay down next to it. Gathering it in her arms, she held it close and rocked it gently. This would be the last time she would hold her lover like this. Perhaps the last time they would even be together.

"What am I to do with you, my love? I can't just leave you here, but I don't know what you want of me."

Burying her face in the gray hair, she let the tears flow, knowing no one was there to see her and witness her weakness, not that she cared. Even a demon could cry.

* * *

Saira could feel the powerful tug pulling her to the Underworld. Apparently Dis needed something, which surprised her. When she arrived, she noticed him pacing back and forth in front of the fireplace.

"Good evening," she said quietly as she shimmered into existence.

"Don't you ever knock?" he growled, irritated that she could come and go without him sensing her.

"And what would you have me knock on? Besides, you obviously wanted to see me or I wouldn't be here."

"Yes, sit," he ordered, motioning to a chair. "I have a dilemma."

"It must be a great one if you're summoning me to help you."

"Believe me, it's not something I wanted."

"I see. So, what can I do for you?"

"I need you to find someone for me."

Saira frowned.

"Find someone? I'm a traveler, not a detective."

"Well, it's your traveler skills that will help find her."

"Her?"

"Yes. A soul. It seems it has been misplaced."

"Misplaced? How can a soul be misplaced and what does that have to do with me?"

"Perhaps it's more accurate to say lost, and one of my demons is on the warpath. If it doesn't show up soon, I'm afraid she'll do something stupid and then I'll be forced to do something I might regret."

"Well, this definitely sounds serious. We can't have the Underlord developing a conscience, now, can we?"

Giving her a wry look, Dis rolled his eyes.

"Are you going to help me or not?"

"I don't even know what you want. How do I know if I am?"

"Fair enough! I need you to follow my demon's timeline. It will lead you to this mortal she's become enamored with. Perhaps once you meet her, you can find where her soul went. It never made it to Soulkeeper."

"What about your Twin's realm?"

"He doesn't have it. She'd never fit in with his collection of namby-pambies. She should have come here."

"And there's no place else she could have gone?"

"There are other places but it would take too long to check them out and some are unreachable, even for me. I want to know where this soul is and I don't have time to look. Sabnock is impatient when she's on a mission."

He scowled. "Now, will you help or not?"

"I can try. It sounds interesting enough. Where do I meet this Sabnock?"

"She just left. Can't you find her timeline using me?"

Saira was stunned. For Dis to offer her one of his *threads* was an indication of how important this was. It left his entire history open for examination if she chose.

"Of course. I just didn't think you'd want me going that route."

"It's not my preference, but it's the only choice at the moment. I warn you, however, take only that which is Sabnock's. I won't tolerate your intrusion elsewhere."

Nodding, Saira focused on the strands emanating from the Underlord. Ignoring those that had nothing to do with Sabnock, she finally located the most recent and followed it to the present, where she found the demoness lying in bed, cradling the cooling body of a mortal.

Embarrassed at having arrived at such an intimate moment, she felt like a voyeur and then chuckled. That was exactly what she was. Wanting to give them privacy, she decided to leave, but stopped when another woman appeared.

* * *

"She will be misssed," a soft voice whispered near the bed. Looking up, Sabnock saw a blonde woman standing a few feet away. She had brown, golden-speckled eyes.

120

Unblinking elliptical pupils reminded the demoness of a snake.

"Who are you?" she demanded, surprised that she hadn't heard the door open.

"A friend. Consstance wass loved by more than you. One of her kind comess to take her body to itss final ressting place."

"You still haven't said who you are and I won't let just anyone take her."

"Forgive me. I am Sssarpe. Consstance and I met only a short while ago but I resspected her. Jusst as she was your lover, one of her kind iss mine. We will make sure she iss given the honorss she hass earned."

A knock on the door interrupted them. Before Sabnock could stand, a dark-skinned woman with pale blue eyes walked in. Walking over to Sarpe, she gave her a quick kiss and then turned to look at the soldier next to Constance.

"I'm Ekimmu," she said, holding out her hand. Sabnock reluctantly shook it, not sure what was going on. "We're sorry to intrude like this, but we must get her body out of here before the hotel people find her."

"You're a Gebian," the demoness said.

"She must have trusted you a lot to tell you about us. Constance wouldn't have disclosed our existence otherwise."

"We were lovers...a long time ago."

Surprised, Ekimmu glanced at Sarpe. When the serpent spirit nodded, confirming the truth, the Gebian gave the demoness a warm smile.

"I'm glad. It's comforting to know she had someone. Now, forgive me, but I don't know your name."

"Sabnock. Lynara Sabnock."

"You belong to Disss," Sarpe accused, moving to stand between Ekimmu and the demoness.

"Belonged! I no longer command his Legions," Sabnock declared, rising to her feet. It was obvious the woman with the strange eyes had taken a dislike to her once she had learned her name.

"Sarpe, love," Ekimmu interrupted. "This isn't the time. Besides, that is none of our business. If Constance loved her, that's all that matters."

Realizing Ekimmu was right, Sarpe backed away.

"You're right, of coursse. I apologize," she said, turning her cold, serpentine eyes on the demoness.

Nodding, Sabnock agreed with the Gebian. If they were her lover's friends, that was all that mattered.

"Where will you take her?"

"Yemaya Lysanne, another friend, has offered her a place amongst her people in the mountains. It is private land and well protected. She will be honored and at peace."

"Lysanne?" Sabnock had heard rumors of the Illusionist's performances but didn't realize she lived in this part of the world.

Ekimmu nodded. "Yes, she and Dakota were very fond of her, too."

"Dakota Devereaux?"

"You know her?"

"No, but Constance wanted me to give her those manuscripts. I promised I would make sure she got them."

"Ah, the history of my people. If you trust me, I will take them to her."

"It would probably be best."

Stepping close to Sarpe, she looked deeply into her eyes, curious about her strange looks. When their gazes locked, the demoness' suspicions were confirmed. Although human in appearance, the woman wasn't, nor was she Gebian or demon.

"What are you?"

Sarpe was amused.

"I'd have thought you would have guesssed by now," she mused. "Neither human nor demon, what iss left?"

"I don't like games," Sabnock growled.

Shaking her head, Ekimmu decided there was too much immortal female estrogen going on.

"Sarpe, be nice."

The spirit made a wry face but relented.

"Ass you wish. I'm a sspirit. My kin are sserpentss," she admitted.

"And Constance knew this?"

"Of course," Ekimmu said.

"I know so little about her. Two weeks was all we had."

"Apparently it wass enough to fall in love. What elsse is there to know?"

"Everything, but I'm too late. I've lost her forever."

"Can you not join her in your realm?" Sarpe asked.

"I tried. I promised her we would be together, but she's not there."

"She didn't come to the ssspirit world. What about the Twin'sss?"

"Dis said she wasn't there."

"And you believe him?" Sarpe asked.

"He would never lie to me about this."

"Then she musst have gone to the Great Beyond," the spirit said. "It is where some sssouls go, although why, we don't know."

"Then I'll go there and get her back," Sabnock vowed.

"First, I suggest we take care of her mortal remains. We need to get her out of here," said Ekimmu.

"Tell me where to take her and I'll have her there in seconds."

Ekimmu gave her directions.

Taking Constance in her arms, Sabnock cradled the body as if it were a child and then disappeared.

"You had better let Yemaya and Dakota know she'ss on her way," Sarpe said.

Ekimmu made a quick call to the Illusionist and her partner. Yemaya promised she would take care of things discreetly.

"You want to ride with me or pull the disappearing act?" Ekimmu asked.

"I'll keep you company, of coursse."

Gathering up the rest of Constance's belongings and making sure there was no evidence of her having stayed there, the two departed. The hotel clerk would figure the old woman had checked out early.

By finding Sabnock, Saira had hoped to locate her lover's *thread* and follow it to its final destination. Unfortunately, the link between the two had somehow been severed, making it impossible to trace. The only way to re-establish it was for the Traveler to journey backward in time and locate the moment they had first met. Then she could follow it forward and reconnect the damaged strands. For the first time, Saira understood her importance. Intunecat was partially right. She was a weaver, mending the damaged *threads* that held the web of time together.

Saira followed the *thread* through hundreds of lives, searching for a clue to Constance's disappearance. For the most part, the demoness' lives or identities were short, lasting only a few years, but occasionally she managed to live longer. Only a few times did she make it beyond a decade. Then humans grew suspicious of Sabnock when she showed no signs of aging. Saira began to understand the demoness better. She chose the most dangerous occupations, assuring her a short existence. The Traveler grabbed one of the longer *threads*, curious because they were different.

CHAPTER 10

LUBRETTE KNEW that as a woman she would have a difficult time being accepted by the American soldiers, even though her skills as a mercenary were impeccable. Had it not been for Major Stanley, she wouldn't even be here. She first met him in Da Nang at a local whorehouse.

Lubrette instantly recognized him as an American Army officer. The short hair and the way he walked would have been enough, but it was the way he spoke that cinched it. Well educated, he was out of place at the dark, smoky brothel, especially since it was obvious he was there for the same thing the enlisted men were, cheap sex.

Watching him through the haze, she wondered what would bring a young officer to such a sleazy place when he could find plenty of beautiful women at the exclusive clubs that had sprung up for those with money. The night she first noticed him, he had ordered a glass of the home brew and looked around.

Seeing all the chairs taken and not wanting to mingle with the locals or the few enlisted men, he spied the empty chair by a tall redheaded woman. No one seemed anxious to sit next to her so he walked over, curious.

"Is this seat taken?" he asked her, his voice raised so she could hear him over the raucous laughter and chatter of the customers. Not receiving an immediate answer, he shrugged and turned.

Guess so, he thought.

"It's not."

Looking back he saw her kick the chair toward him and nod.

"Thanks. You sure you don't mind?"

"If I did I'd have let you walk."

Taking her comment as an invitation, he sat down and motioned for a waitress to bring two more drinks.

"I'm surprised you're by yourself," he said, conversationally.

"Why?"

"Women usually don't even come into these types of places, let alone by themselves. You can't be here for the local entertainment."

"Why not?"

"Well, because. You're sure not very talkative are you?"

Even in the dim light, he could tell her eyes were green. At the moment they gave away nothing about what she was thinking.

"I wasn't aware you were looking for someone to talk to."

"Okay. Maybe if I introduce myself...and before you start to think I'm looking for a pickup, I'm not."

"That's good. I'm the wrong person if you are. Men aren't exactly my thing."

"That's fine with me. I'm not into relationships and you don't seem like someone I'd want to have one with anyway. By the way, my name's Gary."

"Lubrette," she said, shaking the hand he had extended toward her.

"Lubrette. Never knew anyone with that name. You French?"

"Why do you ask?"

"No reason, I guess. Just curious. I've noticed there are still quite a few around. I guess they decided to stay after France pulled out of here."

"I guess. You're American, I take it?"

"Yep. One hundred percent."

"So what are you doing in a place like this? You aren't the typical clientele."

Gary shrugged.

"It's safe."

"Safe? Here?"

Laughing, Gary took a swig of beer and choked. Coughing, he wiped his chin with his arm.

"Well, for what I need, yeah."

"You into smack or whores?"

Gary laughed.

"Whores. I don't do drugs."

"You can't get a clean woman with your looks and money?" Lubrette asked, surprised that the young officer would come to this type of place for sex.

"I could. Unfortunately, clean is the one thing I don't want. It's a little late for me now and I'm not about to pass my problem on to someone else, sooo..." Gary shrugged.

"I see. Syph or Hep."

"You don't waste time, do you?"

The woman shrugged.

"Any reason I should?"

"I guess not. Hep C. No cure and most of the women here already have it and probably everything else."

"And the everything else doesn't scare you?"

"Not really. I figure I'm a dead man anyway. If some VC bullet or booby-trap doesn't get me, the Hep will in a few years."

"There's always a chance someone will come up with a cure."

"Well, if they do, then I figure they'll be able to cure everything else too. Anyway, what brings you here? It sure can't be the sex. A woman with your looks can get that anywhere, man or woman."

Lubrette stared at the soldier for a few seconds.

"No. I come here to pick up a job now and then. It's a good spot to make connections."

"What kind of work, if you don't mind me asking?"

"Mercenary. I'm a guide."

"You!" he exclaimed, surprised. "What kind of guide?"

"Whatever kind you need. I know these jungles like you know your hometown. I know every village, every trail, every rat hole."

Lubrette could tell he doubted her.

"You want references? Call Colonel Ingram with the 4th Infantry. He's with Special Ops."

"I know him. Maybe I will. Look, I have to go. Maybe we'll see each other again."

Lubrette doubted it but nodded.

* * *

Four nights later, she was sitting in the same spot, drinking some hooch, when she noticed Gary leaning against the bar talking to three Vietnamese soldiers she recognized. Two of them had accompanied her on several reconnaissance expeditions deep into the jungle. The third she had heard rumors about. He wasn't someone she'd want at her back.

Signaling to a barmaid, she gave her a few bucks and told her to bring Gary to the table. Minutes later, he showed up smiling.

"Hey, how goes it?" he asked.

"Fine. Just thought I'd warn you about one of those fellas you were chatting with."

Looking back at the three men, Gary frowned.

"Word is they can be trusted."

"Two yes, but the one with the scar on his neck is Viet Cong."

"How do you know?"

"I know," Lubrette said, but didn't say anything more.

"Thanks. By the way, Ingram sends his regards."

"Back at him," she replied.

Glancing around the room, Gary looked like he wanted to say something else, but hesitated.

"Listen, we need to talk, but not here."

"Name the place."

"My place and no, this isn't a pick up. I just don't want to talk here."

"Works for me."

Giving her the time and location, Gary left. An hour later, Lubrette followed, making sure she wasn't being followed. The Viet Cong had spies everywhere. Most knew Lubrette Sabnock. More than once, she had been targeted for assassination but had managed to thwart each attempt. The assassins paid dearly for their mistakes.

* * *

Ringing the small bell outside Gary's door, she glanced up and down the hall, checking to see if anyone else was around. At four in the morning, most people were in bed. When Gary answered, he also looked around and then motioned her inside.

"Drink?"

"No thanks. I'm at my limit now. What's up?"

"Straight to the point. I like that. Let me show you something."

Walking to a small makeshift desk, he unrolled a map and pointed to a spot.

"Quang Ngai. You know this province?"

"Yes. Why?"

"Well, we hear that the VC's 48th Battalion is in that area. If we can take them out or at least inflict some serious damage, it'll be a major blow to the Cong. We need several guides who know that area intimately. Ingram said you were the first on his list."

"You want me to find them?"

"Yes and no. We think they've holed up in a small village called Son My. If we can get to them without being discovered, we can surround them and wipe them out."

"And the villagers?"

"We're just after the VC, not civilians," Gary said, sounding indignant.

"Right. Who do you have in the area now?"

"You mean units? The 1st Battalion and 11th Brigade. Why?"

"I've heard rumors about them. They aren't very discreet about their hatred for the VC or anyone else that gets in their way."

Gary nodded. He had also heard about the group, particularly C Company. Ingram had assured him the men were good soldiers as long as someone kept a firm hand on them.

"I'll be heading up this assignment. They'll do as they're ordered and nothing more."

"Okay. How long before we leave?"

"In three days. Meet me at hanger 31 and we'll 'copter to Quang Ngai City. From there we'll finalize everything."

"And who am I suppose to ask for? I'm sure there are a lot of Garys around."

"Oh, right. Major Gary Stanley, Special Ops."

Lubrette left without saying anything else. Gary shook his head and wondered how he was going to introduce the handsome woman to his men. Women were usually considered a liability on the front line.

* * *

When Lubrette arrived at the hanger, she was dressed in green cammies, a utility belt holding two semi-automatics, several clips, a large hunting knife and several small leather cases attached to the belt. Her right boot had another knife sheathed on the outside near her calf. The men would have been surprised at the things they didn't see. Her backpack carried everything needed to take care of wounds, disinfectant, water, and several magazine clips for her M-16A1 rifle, which was strapped to her pack. Food wasn't a problem for her since she could live off the land.

Major Stanley had updated his officers on Lubrette and her credentials. Apparently some had heard of her already and were curious about the woman who was going to help them defeat the VC. The skeptics were quickly silenced by their CO and told to get over it.

The flight to Quang Ngai City took about four hours. From the base they caught two more helicopters to the C Company's camp. Lubrette was introduced to the soldiers that evening after mess. Several of the men protested, declaring they weren't following a woman. Others made the typical male lewd remarks, wanting to impress their buddies. Lubrette took everything in stride, ignoring everyone until one soldier walked up to her and ran his eyes up and down her body as if she were a piece of meat.

"I ain't goin' nowhere with you, except maybe in my bedroll," he said, glancing cockily at his buddies.

Lubrette snorted and turned to walk away. She hated stupidity and was more than willing to let the idiot's arrogance slide. Unfortunately, the soldier was more stupid than she thought. Grabbing her by the shoulder he spun her around and tried to capture her in a crude embrace.

Before he knew what happened, he was lying on the ground on his back, with a knife pressed against his neck. Two men jumped up to rescue him and Lubrette pulled out another knife with her left hand and threw it at one while glaring at the other. Letting out a scream, one of the rescuers found his boot pinned to the ground, the knife imbedded in his foot. Before anyone could react, she had pulled her gun and was pointing it at the second man, her other knife still pressed against her assaulter's neck.

"I wouldn't!" she hissed, her voice low and angry.

"What's going on here?" Major Stanley demanded, walking toward the group of men who were now loudly bitching. Silence fell immediately.

"Nothing," Lubrette said, holstering her gun and sheathing her knife.

Standing, she brushed her pants off and walked away.

133

Several minutes later, Gary caught up to her and handed her the second knife.

"I think you lost this," he said, guessing at what had happened. None of the men wanted to talk about being bested by a woman.

"Thanks."

"I'm not sure how it got into Kappleman's boot, but he's going to be out of commission for a few days."

"Accidents happen."

"Yeah. Well, hopefully, there won't be any others. We need everyone we can get."

"Guess it's up to the guys to watch themselves then."

"I hear you. We'll be moving out tomorrow. Do you need anything?"

"No. Just make sure we have plenty of ammunition. I don't want us to come up short if we get trapped somewhere."

"I thought it was your job to keep that from happening," Gary teased.

"I'm a scout and guide, not God."

"Too bad. I have a feeling we could use him about now."

Major Gary Stanley didn't know how prophetic his words would turn out to be.

CHAPTER 11

LUBRETTE HAD been to Quang Ngai several times. It was normally a quiet place. The villagers spent most of the time growing rice and tending their livestock. If the VC were hiding in Quang Ngai, there was nothing the people could do to stop them. The Viet Cong were notorious for their brutality.

Pointing to the map on the board, she quickly outlined the topography of the area, making sure the unit commanders knew the locations most likely to be booby-trapped and the ones they could pass through with little resistance. Pointing to the rice fields, she explained they would be the easiest spot to begin the assault.

Taking over the meeting, Major Stanley asked if there were any questions.

"Good," he said when no one said anything. "Now, I want you to go in there fast and hard. Make sure the men take out any VC. Don't chase them into the jungles, don't leave any shack unchecked...and be careful. These guys are good. They are experts at booby-traps. Finally, I don't want any civilians harmed if possible. We are here to fight the Cong, not the villagers."

"Look Major, the men can't be expected to mollycoddle villagers now."

"I didn't say mollycoddle, Sergeant. I said our targets are the VC. Are you having a problem understanding the difference?"

"No sir."

"Good. Now, move out."

Lubrette knew about warfare. She had fought in so many battles, she understood and recognized the telltale signs of men on the verge of losing control. C Company was almost there.

"I hope your NCOs keep a strong grip on your men, Gary," she said after everyone had left. "One mistake and this could get ugly."

"They're good men, Lubrette. Trust me on this."

Lubrette did trust him, but she knew he had put too much trust in his soldiers. Once this was over with, hopefully they would be reassigned and fresh troops brought in.

* * *

With orders to move in rapidly and secure the area as quickly as possible, C Company arrived at the outskirts of the village around 0730. Offloading, they spread out and headed for the village. Everyone was pumped for the fight, hoping to kill as many VC as possible. A few days before, several of their men had been killed in an ambush and the soldiers were looking for revenge. Given the right incentive, they intended on getting it.

* * *

"Out! Out! Out!" Major Stanley yelled, signaling for the soldiers to leave the helicopter after he and Lubrette had jumped from the platform. Spreading out, everyone crouched down and waited until all of the men were on the ground. Raising his arm, he waved them forward. Minutes later, an elderly man came running toward them, his arms waving in the air. Before the major could send someone to see what was up, a shot was fired and the villager fell.

"Who the hell fired that shot?" he yelled angrily.

No one answered. Shaking his head, he looked at Lubrette, wanting to reassure her it had been an accident. Deep down he knew better and felt uncomfortable, hoping it wasn't a sign of things to come.

* * *

Lubrette wasn't surprised when things started to go horribly wrong. She had sensed the deep-seated anger in several of the men. It was like a virus and almost no one was immune. The raid on the village was a failure. The VC had received word of the coming attack and had disappeared into the jungles, leaving only the villagers and some booby-traps behind to greet the Americans.

Killing the old man was the first step down a short path to devastation. Several minutes later, other villagers who had run out to see what was happening were slaughtered. Terrified, the rest hid in their huts. Frustrated the soldiers began firing rounds into the huts, killing anything and everything they saw. Men, women, children, it didn't make any difference.

"I don't know what to do," Gary said, turning to Lubrette for guidance.

"There's nothing to do," she replied. "They're beyond listening to you. These aren't men anymore. They're animals."

"They're soldiers," he cried. "They're trained to obey."

"They were never soldiers. These men are brutes. It was only a matter of time before they reverted to their true nature. I'm surprised you didn't see it."

"No!" Gary said, refusing to believe it. "No!"

Running toward a small group who had pushed a woman down on the ground, he grabbed one by the shoulder and pulled him away.

"Stop it! You have your orders," he yelled, stepping between the woman and the soldiers.

"Get out of the way, Major," one of them growled.

"No. This stops now."

Pushing past him, the soldier began removing his utility belt. Gary lunged at him and pulled him backward. Without thinking, the soldier pulled his knife and stabbed the major in the stomach. Stunned, Gary looked down at the knife and then back at the man. Clutching his stomach, he fell to his knees and tumbled onto his side. Seconds later, a shot rang out and the killer collapsed next to him.

Turning to see who had shot their companion, the remainder of the men saw Lubrette standing several meters away holding her rifle. Before they could react, she opened fire and killed them all. Afterward, she motioned for the villager to run away and then knelt next to Gary.

"I...I thought they...were...sol...diers," he gasped. "We...were sup...posed to be...better...better."

Holding his head on her lap, Lubrette looked at the carnage around them. Shaking her head, she wanted to tell him he was a fool, but realized it would serve no purpose. He already knew that.

"War brings out the worst in us," she said softly, stroking his hair.

The sound of a helicopter caught her attention. Turning in that direction, she noticed one of the pilots had positioned the vehicle between some villagers and the soldiers. The crewmen had their guns pointed at the Americans, threatening to shoot if any more civilians were attacked.

Holding Gary up so he could see, she pointed to the helicopter.

"Look. There are your soldiers, Gary."

It was the last thing Gary saw before he died. Lowering him to the ground, Lubrette stood and disappeared into the jungles. For the first time in her many lives, she walked away from a fight.

The soldiers never knew what happened to Lubrette Sabnock. The men involved in the incident were afraid if word got out about the incident they would be court-martialed. It was in their best interest not to mention the female scout and so no record of her participation was ever entered into the records. Once they returned to base, a few tried to find her, hoping to make sure she didn't open her mouth. After several months and no success, they assumed she had either been killed or captured by the VC.

Gary Stanley's body was returned to the states to be buried in Arlington National Cemetery with full honors. His parents were informed that he had been killed in action and presented with several medals honoring his sacrifice. No one noticed the tall, redheaded woman standing several feet away from the friends and family until after the services were over. When she turned to leave, Gary's mother walked over, curious about the stranger.

"Excuse me," she said, her voice trembling slightly. "Did you know my son?"

The woman stopped and turned.

"Yes. He was a good man and a good soldier. Someone to be proud of."

Mrs. Stanley gave a weak smile.

"I know. Gary always had a sense of duty. He hated this war but...well, you know how it is. We raised him to be proud of his country. I just wish we knew how he was killed. No one will talk about it."

"He died saving a villager. He believed it was his job to protect the innocent."

Tears streamed down his mother's cheeks. Taking the stranger's hand, she clasped it tightly.

"Thank you," she whispered. "I'm sorry. I didn't get your name."

"Lubrette Sabnock."

Had Mrs. Stanley looked behind her, she would have seen several soldiers stiffen when they heard the name. Fearfully, they glanced at the woman with the angry eyes. As if an illusion, those who had participated in the slaughter saw the color change from an angry green to a raging dark brown. Some imagined they saw flames burning brightly within the darkened pupils and swallowed nervously. Dropping their gazes, they suddenly had a feeling they had looked into the fires of Hell. When they glanced up again, Lubrette smiled and walked away, knowing they had.

Saira shook her head and moved on. She never understood humanity's need for war. For all the pain and suffering, it rarely solved anything. Traveling backward in time, she stopped to observe another of Sabnock's lives.

CHAPTER 12

SHE WAS AN anomaly more than capable of holding her own in battle. Perhaps that was why the braves never complained. Or maybe they were just afraid of her. It was rare that a woman was allowed into the circle of warriors.

From the moment she had arrived in their village, she had established herself as equal to their bravest and most skilled. Although they didn't know from where she came, nor did they care, they were curious about her skills in fighting, weaponry and especially in handling the wild ponies they captured and trained for battle.

It was early in the spring of 1869 when she rode into the village on a coal black horse. Dressed in a deerskin top and loin cloth with a bow and quiver of arrows strapped across her back, she looked stoically at the squaws and children who watched curiously from their tents. The braves had been aware of her approach for several minutes, having been warned in advance by their lookouts. Now they waited to see this intruder who dared enter their small community uninvited.

Stopping just short of the chief's teepee, the woman dismounted, looking neither left nor right. She knew that to do so would reduce her to the level of squaw in the tribe and make it more difficult to be accepted as an equal to the men.

* * *

Minikajau was enjoying freshly roasted rabbit and rattlesnake when one of his braves informed him of the woman's approach. As the son of Crazy Horse, he was in charge of the village while his father was away. The Lakota grand council had called a meeting of all the tribes to discuss the new treaty agreed upon by Red Cloud and the Great White Father.

Although quiet and reserved, Minikajau was highly respected by the members of his tribe. His prowess in battle and common sense approach to problems made him a good leader. He was the voice of reason when it came to settling disputes between warriors or tribes.

The soft sound of horse steps brought him to his feet. Pushing aside the colored fabric draped across the opening of the teepee, he stepped into the cool morning sun and watched the strange-looking woman approach. Red hair was virtually unheard of among the Indian nations. For a woman to wear hers so short reminded him of some of the white men who were now invading his land. Her copper-colored skin glistened in the light.

When she was close enough for him to get a good look, he realized she had a fine coat of golden hair on her arms and legs. Watching her dismount and ignore the others of his tribe as if they didn't exist was impressive and showed bravery, he unconsciously nodded his approval.

When the woman turned from her pony and made eye contact with him, Minikajau's eyes widened in surprise.

Pale green eyes stared unblinkingly at him. He would have sworn he saw fires burning deep within the pupils. Shaking his head slightly, he told himself it must be the sun's reflection.

* * *

Walking to stand in front of the young chieftain, the woman raised her right hand, palm up.

"Hau, Kola!" she said using the traditional Lakota greeting.

"Hau," Minikajau replied, startled that a female would greet him in such a manner. He was not willing to call her friend, as her greeting implied. To do so would make it appear that he accepted her as an equal. As impressive as she looked, it didn't make her anything other than a woman at the moment, even if she did capture and hold his gaze as a warrior would do.

"Do you understand the white man's tongue?" she asked.

"I understand it. You do not look like white woman."

"I am what I am."

"You are brave or stupid to come here alone."

"The Lakota are an honorable people. I'm not in any danger."

Minikajau was surprised that the intruder had not referred to them as Sioux. It was the white man's word for the Lakota and considered an insult by the people of the Lakota Nation.

"You are a fool," he replied, instantly dismissing her as weak minded. Even his bravest warrior knew he could be killed by another tribe or a white man trespassing on his sacred land. Turning, he signaled to one of his braves to remove her.

Little Deer grinned at the thought of taking the woman to his teepee. She was handsome and looked strong. He needed a squaw to do his cooking and bear him children. Walking up to her, he strutted around her like a proud peacock, wanting to impress her with his good looks and physique. When she ignored him, he stopped in front of her and glared, hoping to scare her. Still she ignored him.

"You come," he ordered, motioning for her to follow.

"No," she replied, making eye contact for the first time.

Little Deer saw the flames burning in her eyes and stepped back, not sure what he should do. Although he feared no man, he believed strongly in the spirits and recognized she was more than just a woman.

Seeing the confused look on his warrior's face, Minikajau frowned.

"Is she not to your liking?" he asked Little Deer.

"What he likes or not has nothing to do with me," the woman replied, stoically. "He knows I will kill him if he touches me."

The young chieftain laughed, appreciating her brave words even if she was a fool. Motioning to two more braves, he ordered them to take her. As they moved forward, the woman removed her bow and arrows and laid them on the ground, then faced them.

Pulling a knife from its scabbard, she flexed her shoulders and then bent her knees slightly and waited. The two braves looked at each other, amused. It had been awhile since they had captured a fiery female and they looked forward to the entertainment.

Circling her, one signaled for the other to go for her legs, while he would grab her higher up. Launching themselves simultaneously, they were stunned to find themselves lying on the ground, one on top of the other. The woman stood next to them smiling.

Although Minikajau kept his stoic expression, he laughed inwardly. The woman had managed to sidestep the two braves at the last moment. There was no question she was fast. Climbing to their feet, the warriors again circled and lunged. Again, they missed.

"Is this the best you have, Minikajau?"

The inferred insult quickly dispelled the leader's humor. Signaling for the warriors to back away, he stepped forward. It was up to him to show his people why he would one day be their chief. Circling her, he watched her fluid movement and realized she moved easily, like a mountain lion.

After making several feints in her direction, he dove at her and wrapped his arms around her waist. The two fell to the ground and began wrestling for dominance. It was then Minikajau realized she was extremely strong, stronger than a woman should be.

Wondering if she was a spirit sent to test him, he struggled hard to subdue her. As they rolled across the ground, the Indians watching moved out of the way, not wanting to get caught up in the battle.

Once, while the two combatants' heads were close together, the woman pressed her lips against his ear and whispered.

"It wouldn't be good for a future chief to be beaten by a woman."

Minikajau blinked at her audacity.

"I think I will keep you for myself when we are done," he replied.

"Or I will keep you for myself," she countered, licking his ear.

Furious at the insult, he renewed his efforts, only to have them thwarted by her agility in slipping from his grasp. Jumping up, she backed off and laughed softly.

The Indians watching the fight became nervous. Their chieftain was a skilled warrior. For a woman to beat him would bring dishonor on him and the tribe, unless she was more than a woman.

Minikajau knew he had a problem. If this woman defeated him, he would no longer be their leader or sit on the tribal council. He wondered if she was a spirit. If so, he realized he had no chance in winning the fight. Still, he was a warrior. Losing was not an option.

Rushing her, he again wrapped his arms around her waist and tried to pull her off her feet. Making eye contact, he found himself drowning in the fiery flames burning in their depths.

"You are a spirit," he growled.

Falling to the ground, she again leaned close to his ear.

"Perhaps...or perhaps I'm just a woman who fights better than you. Decide now what you want...to lead your people or to be led by someone less than you."

Minikajau was torn. To give up would make him weak but to be beaten by a woman would be a disgrace.

Recognizing his dilemma, the woman grabbed his shoulders and rolled onto her back, giving him the advantage. Immediately, Minikajau realized what she had done and pressed his weight on her chest while pushing his elbow against her neck. The glint in her eyes told him she wasn't afraid or defeated. She had willingly allowed him to win so he could retain the respect of his people and his position as their leader.

Pushing away from her, he stood and stepped back.

"What is your name?" he asked, motioning for two braves to pull her up.

"Tanc," she replied, jumping to her feet before the men touched her.

"Tanc. It is a strange name. Why are you here, Tanc?"

"I came to help you fight the white man."

Minikajau was stunned. The thought of a woman fighting with his warriors was unimaginable.

"Women don't fight."

"Maybe yours don't, but where I come from, we do. Do I need to prove myself to you?"

"No. You will prove yourself worthy to my braves. If they agree, then I will think about it."

"Fair enough. How do I do this?"

"You fight well but you must prove your skills with the knife, the bow and arrow and riding."

Picking up her knife, which had been intentionally discarded during the fight, she flipped it around in her hand and then threw it at a pole thirty paces away. When it stuck between the eyes of a deer skull, everyone gasped. Walking over to her bow and arrows, she pulled one of the arrows from the quiver, notched it and fired the shaft at the same skull. The tip penetrated the skull less than a finger's width from the knife.

Impressed, Minikajau nodded his head in approval. Even his best braves couldn't match that.

"What would you like me to do to prove my riding skills?"

Suspecting it would be a waste of time, he told her she had to race three of his best warriors to the edge of the village, circle it once and return to his teepee. Once everyone was mounted he gave the signal.

Within minutes, Tanc had returned. Her black pony seemed as fresh as when she had started. The woman smiled faintly but didn't say anything. Sheepishly, the three braves pulled up seconds later, jumped off their ponies and walked over to examine hers.

"I will trade you three ponies for him," one offered.

"I will give you five," another one said.

"He's not for sale," Tanc said.

"Then I will take him from you," threatened the first, angry that a woman had bested him and then dared to deny him the pony.

"You'll die trying," she replied calmly, her gaze challenging him.

Puffing out his chest, Brave Eagle tried to stare her down but failed.

"Enough," Minikajau said. He had no doubt the woman could and would kill Brave Eagle if the situation escalated.

Surprised, the brave looked at his leader. When he was motioned to step back, he gave the woman a threatening look, warning her that the dispute wasn't over yet.

Tanc grinned, which caused the warrior Brave Eagle to blush, humiliated that his people had witnessed her defiance.

The braves who had been watching the exchange began teasing the young brave good-naturedly, but Tanc knew there would be problems later if she didn't do something.

"Brave Eagle, I noticed your pony is well-trained. She responds quickly to your signals, which are barely noticeable. Did you train her yourself?"

Straightening his shoulders, the Indian nodded his head once.

"White Dove is smart. She learn quickly," he said, proudly.

"Can you help me with Demon? He can be stubborn sometimes."

Brave Eagle looked at her suspiciously. Her pony's responses were quick and precise. Still, if the woman wanted his help, it would improve his standing with the others, who had grown quiet while they listened to the exchange.

"I will help."

"Good. I will pay you by letting Demon breed with White Dove. You may keep the offspring."

Brave Eagle's eyes opened wide in shock. The other warriors and the villagers looked at each other, surprised by the offer. Minikajau barely hid his smile. He realized the woman had just sealed her position as a member of the tribe and as a warrior with his braves. Brave Eagle was very influential among his men. Having his mare breed with the magnificent black stallion would increase both his status and his loyalty to Tanc.

Turning to the chieftain, Tanc waited for him to put the question to the braves. Minikajau debated on how long to make her wait but realized they would probably stand there all day.

"Men of the Lakota Nation, do you accept this woman as your brother in battle?"

Several seconds of silence followed and then Brave Eagle raised his arm and let out a whoop. Startled, the other braves looked at him and he nodded. One by one, each of the Indians raised an arm and yelled until the entire group of warriors could be heard voicing their approval.

"Good." Pointing to several teepees, he told her to choose whichever one she wanted. "You may take one of the unmarried squaws to cook and clean for you."

"I won't need one," Tanc replied. "I do my own work."

Minikajau frowned. Braves didn't do that type of work. Still, he had a dilemma. Tanc was a woman, also.

"You are a brave now. You must take a squaw. It dishonors our people for a warrior to cook or clean."

Tanc sighed. The last thing she wanted was a woman servant, but tribal customs were important.

"Fine, but she will only cook. I clean my own buckskins."

Accepting the compromise, the chieftain nodded. He had no doubts that this would not be the first one with this woman.

CHAPTER 1 3

TANC SETTLED easily into the ways of the Lakota. Riding with the men on hunting excursions and scouting trips to see how many whites were intruding into their territory became a regular routine. On the days they stayed near the village, the warriors would practice hand-to-hand warfare tactics or perfect their expertise with their weapons.

It was then that Tanc gained the respect of the braves the most. She would teach them techniques in fighting and bareback riding to improve their survival in battles. Soon the braves gained a formidable reputation among the other tribes, providing them with a degree of protection from attack, at least from other Indians.

For the first few years, several of the braves tried to win her favor, hoping to bed her. One by one, they eventually gave up and good-naturedly teased her about her celibate life.

"It has been two years since you arrived here," Little Deer pointed out after returning from a buffalo hunt. "Don't you miss being with a man?"

Tanc looked at him and raised both eyebrows, questioningly.

"I thought braves were men. Have I missed something?"

"You know what I mean. Why haven't you chosen a mate? There are plenty of young braves who would love the honor."

"I'm not interested in a mate," Tanc said, pulling out her knife for sharpening.

"How will you bear children, if you don't mate?" Little Deer asked, frowning. All women wanted children, he thought.

"Except me," Tanc replied to his unspoken words. Unconsciously, her eyes began following a young Indian woman recently captured on a raiding party.

Little Deer shook his head. She always seemed to know what he was thinking. He was about to comment when he noticed her eyes following the captive's movements. It had never dawned on him that Tanc would be interested in women. Now it made sense.

"You like her?" he asked, motioning toward the woman as she disappeared inside of Gray Cloud's tent.

Tanc looked at Little Deer, not sure how to respond.

Nodding his head, her friend grinned.

"You like her," he said, answering his own question. "Why don't you take her? Gray Cloud doesn't deserve her."

"She is his. He found her."

"He treats her badly. Already she bears the scars of his rage."

As if to prove his point, Tanc saw the woman's body thrown out of the tent followed by Gray Cloud, who was carrying a leather whip. When he began beating her, Tanc and Little Deer jumped up and ran over to intervene.

"What are you doing?" Little Deer demanded, disgusted.

153

"She is lazy. I'm teaching her a lesson," the Indian snarled.

"Beating her will only teach her hatred. She is like a young mare. You must use gentle hands if you want to train her properly."

"Bah," Gray Cloud growled. "You are soft. A firm hand is all it takes."

Pulling back his arm for another strike, he was surprised when Tanc stepped between him and his prize.

"That is enough," she said quietly.

Enraged, the Indian swung the whip at her, catching her left cheek. Blood poured from the split skin but Tanc didn't flinch or make a sound. Only her eyes betrayed the fury raging inside. Gray Cloud swallowed nervously and stepped back, knowing he would pay dearly for the blunder.

"I'll sell her to you," he offered, his voice shaking slightly.

"What is your price?"

Glancing at Little Deer, Gray Cloud realized he had better make a generous offer.

"Two ponies...young ponies."

"No," Tanc said, surprising both braves.

"It's a fair price," he said gruffly.

"No ponies. No animals. You have no respect for them."

Gray Cloud was at a loss now. There was nothing else he needed.

"What do you want?" he asked, his eyes begging her to come up with something that would help him save face.

"I'll take her off your hands. You say she is lazy. Why would you want a lazy squaw? She will cook your meals and wash your clothes, but she stays in my teepee."

Realizing he had no choice, Gray Cloud willingly agreed.

Helping the woman to her feet, Tanc pointed to her tent and nodded. Turning back to Gray Cloud, she let him feel the full force of her anger with her next words.

"And Gray Cloud, if you ever strike her again, I will kill you."

Gray Cloud nodded, knowing it was not an idle threat.

"You're lucky she didn't do it tonight," Little Deer said.

"Over a squaw?"

"Over this woman. Tanc has taken a liking to her."

Gray Cloud looked at the brave, confused. Laughing, Little Deer just shook his head and walked away. How a brave could be such a good warrior and so dumb was a mystery.

Slipping inside the tent, Tanc saw the woman trying to clean the slashes on her back. Taking the cloth from her hand, she dipped it in water and then began wiping the blood away. Before she could say anything, the entrance curtain was pushed aside and Little Deer walked in carrying a small bowl.

"I thought you might need this," he said, handing it to her. "The Shaman gave it to me. He said to rub it on the wound and it will heal quickly."

"Thanks, Little Deer."

Feeling awkward, the brave put the bowl next to them and left. Scooping up some of the poultice, she patted it on the wounds and then pulled the sleeve back on the woman's shoulder. Afterward, she slid over onto her bed of skins, put her arm over her face and closed her eyes, giving the woman privacy. Moments later, she heard the woman moving and then a hand gently clasped her arm and pulled it down. Tanc stared into her eyes looking for something, what, she didn't know. When the woman started cleaning the slashed cheek, she remained still, showing no sign of pain.

"What's your name?" Tanc asked softly.

"Raven."

"Thank you, Raven."

That night Raven curled up close to Tanc for warmth and comfort.

CHAPTER 1 4

IN TIME, Raven and Tanc grew comfortable with each other. Tanc provided her food and protection and Raven prepared Tanc's meals, washed and mended her clothes and took care of her injuries, which were rare.

After the run-in with Gray Cloud, Tanc had moved Raven into her own tent, but kept her word to Gray Cloud. Raven would perform the normal duties expected of a brave's woman – with one exception. Gray Cloud was forbidden to touch her. Tanc had made herself clear on that matter.

One night, during an especially cold winter, Raven developed a fever. Delirious and shivering, she clung to Tanc's body, trying desperately to warm her own. It was one of the few times the demoness broke her vows and turned up her body temperature enough to comfort the woman.

Raven awoke slowly, trying to remember what had happened. Opening her eyes, she stared into the first green eyes she had ever seen. Within their depths, she would have sworn she saw fires blazing.

"How are you feeling?" Tanc asked.

"Better," Raven said, feeling shy.

"Good. You were very sick and cold."

"I don't remember." Raven shifted slightly, not sure what else to say.

"Are you well enough to get up?"

"Yes," Raven replied and started to move.

"No, stay," Tanc said. "I was just asking."

Smiling, Raven settled back on the animal skins and reached up to run her finger down the scar on the demoness' cheek.

"Does it bother you?" Raven asked.

"No."

"Do you mind me touching you like this?" she whispered.

"No."

"You don't talk much, do you?"

"No," Tanc said and then smiled.

"That's fine. I can talk enough for both of us."

Tanc laughed. Raven rarely spoke.

"So I've noticed," she teased.

"Do you like me?" Raven asked, boldly, finding the warrior pleasing to look at.

"Of course, otherwise, I would have sold you a long time ago," Tanc replied, deliberately misunderstanding the question.

"No, I mean do you *like* me? Do you like women?"

"Yes. I like women. Why do you ask?"

Raven sighed.

"Do you want me...like a man would want me?"

Tanc examined the woman's face. A relationship would complicate her life, but she wasn't immune to desire. It was the one emotion demons understood well.

"Yes."

"Then why haven't you taken me before now? Any other brave would have."

"I don't take women against their will."

"And if they want you to take them? Have you slept with other women in this village?"

"No."

Raven sat up and slowly pulled her deerskin shirt off.

"Then take me," she whispered, her voice husky with desire. Tanc gently pushed her down onto the furs and moved over her, pinning her arms above her head with one hand. She ran her other hand over the young woman's body, enjoying the feel of the soft skin.

Stroking the breasts with her fingertips, she marveled at how the nipples pebbled when aroused. Already, she could smell the musky odor of Raven's arousal. Inhaling deeply, she could feel the heat building inside of her own body. Realizing the human body could never tolerate the full impact of her passion, she cooled the fires raging inside of her.

As her free hand roamed slowly up and down Raven's body, she leaned down and stroked the woman's stomach with her tongue. Raven arched her back, trying to pull her own hands free so she could touch her warrior. Tanc increased her grip slightly.

"No," she ordered and then smiled.

Taking a nipple between her teeth, she pulled lightly, making sure not to cause pain. When Raven gasped, she released it and repeated the process on the other. Tanc enjoyed foreplay, especially drawing it out as long as possible. By the time she had finished teasing Raven with her tongue and fingers, the woman was writhing uncontrollably.

"Roll over," she ordered. Raven instantly obeyed. Running her palms over the woman's bare butt, she leaned down. "You are my woman now, not just in name."

Raven nodded.

Running her fingers between the young squaw's thighs, she teased the coarse hairs and then nudged the lips apart and inserted two fingers into her slick opening. Moving her hand in and out, slowly at first, she picked up the rhythm.

Her face buried in the furs, Raven tried desperately to push upward, wanting to match her warrior's movements. She had been with men before but had never felt so aroused. Even her body juices felt unusually warm.

Tanc made sure she cooled the tender skin as her lover's fluids boiled and vaporized. Humans were incapable of withstanding the full force of a demon's passions. Tanc could inflame them to heights unimaginable and she did.

Orgasm followed orgasm until Raven was so exhausted she thought she'd die. Finally taking pity on her, Tanc ceased her lovemaking and began gently massaging Raven's spent muscles. Once she had relaxed, they fell asleep together.

* * *

Tanc was aware of Little Deer entering the tent but was too comfortable to wake up. Finding his friend sleeping soundly, Little Deer decided that he and the other braves could do without her this one time. There was plenty of game near the village. They would bring her some of the best cuts of meat, just as she had done for them in the past.

For seven years, the lovers stayed together, sharing a teepee. Raven was happy, knowing she was loved by one of the Lakota's best warriors, while Tanc was content to let her believe it. Both knew it couldn't last forever. Neither knew the end would arrive so soon.

* * *

The white men were like a plague, encroaching further and further onto the lands that the Lakota had been promised by the Treaty of 1868. That document had guaranteed the Indians' sacred grounds would remain unsettled and untouched.

With the discovery of gold, it became clear that the treaty wouldn't last. More and more settlements were established and more clashes occurred between settlers and Indians. Eventually the Lakota, united with the Cheyenne, left their reservations, traveling deep into the Black Hills. After several council meetings they decided to take back what was rightfully theirs.

The U.S. Cavalry, in order to force the natives back onto their reservations, sent several units out to capture the rebellious Sioux. Each time, they were defeated. Finally, fearing a complete uprising, Washington dispatched a large contingent of soldiers to take control of the situation.

Lt. Colonel George Custer saw this as a great opportunity to rise higher in the ranks. Being ambitious, he knew it could eventually lead to a run for the presidency.

* * *

Tanc sat quietly, listening to the chiefs and their lieutenants as they discussed future plans. Already the white soldiers were gathered in the foothills, their numbers increasing daily. Several of the tribal elders called for peace talks with the Great White Father. Red Cloud, who had won a victory for his people in the Treaty of 1868 wanted to try one more time for a peaceful settlement. Many of the tribal groups agreed with him.

* * *

"Fighting will gain us nothing but sorrow and tears." Red Cloud said. "We must settle this with words, not by bow and arrow."

"The white man's words are false. You know this better than any here, Red Cloud. Have they not broken the other treaties, already? Their soldiers no longer try to keep the settlers off our land or our sacred soil. Already, they destroy our land looking for gold," Crazy Horse replied. "We must show them our strength."

"There is strength in words. Let us try."

"Bah!" Sitting Bull declared. "They do not understand words. They only understand force. My people will not be led from our lands like children. The Great White Father does not care that our women and children starve because our buffalo are slaughtered. He does not care that his own people have broken the treaties. The settlers take our land for their own and we are expected to accept this. I say *no more!*

Several braves cheered his words.

The debate went on for several days. Eventually, Red Cloud left with his followers, leaving Sitting Bull and Crazy Horse behind.

* * *

"What do you think?" Brave Eagle asked, chewing on a piece of deer jerky.

Tanc shrugged. She already knew how Crazy Horse felt. Minikajau had talked to her many times about his father's thoughts.

"I'm just a warrior," she said. "I don't question my leaders."

Brave Eagle snorted.

"Since when? You are always challenging them."

Tanc grinned. It was true. Had she been just a squaw, they would have traded her a long time ago. As one of their best warriors, they knew better. No one wanted her training other tribes.

"You know what I mean. I leave the big decisions to the chiefs and the war council."

"You're good at evading the question."

"Okay. I think we are going to war and we'll lose."

"You think the white man fights better than us?"

"No, I think they outnumber us. They'll wear us down. Many braves will die. Eventually there will be no one left to fight and then our people will be forced back onto the reservations and forgotten."

"Then why do we bother to fight?"

"Because we have no choice. It's better to fight and be remembered for our bravery, then submit, knowing our children's children will call us weak."

CHAPTER 15

IT WAS THE spring of 1876. Many of the tribes had joined forces and set up camp in the Big Horn Valley. For several moons, they lived peacefully, hoping they would be left alone. When Minikajau learned that some rogue Indians had murdered several settlers, he knew the soldiers would be coming.

Then one morning, several braves charged into the village with news that an army had crossed the Rosebud River.

"Did you see who leads them?" Minikajau asked.

"Yellow Hair."

Nodding, the chieftain sent for Tanc and Brave Eagle.

"Choose your bravest warriors and focus on Yellow Hair. He must be destroyed."

"Wouldn't it be better to capture him?"

Minikajau rejected the idea. Better to destroy the enemy now than take a chance on him returning with more soldiers.

"No, we must send the Great White Father a strong message. We won't be forced from these sacred grounds."

"More will come," Tanc reasoned.

"Then more will die. Now go, and may the spirits watch over you!"

* * *

Sitting Bull and Crazy Horse had planned for this moment. They had deliberately divided their numbers into small groups and ordered them to stay inside the tents during the day, hoping the white man's scouts wouldn't realize how many warriors were gathered. It worked.

When Custer received word of the encampment, he saw a chance to make a name for himself. If he could surprise the Indians, he was sure he could defeat them and break the back of the Sioux Nation. The colonel was known for his over-confidence and arrogance.

On June 25th, leading the 7th Calvary, he came upon an Indian camp. Only the Rosebud River stood between him and his target. Hoping to do a night crossing, he was quickly discouraged by his scouts, who informed him that it would be impossible. Eventually, he conceded and ordered his soldiers to cross at sunrise. They were spotted by several Sioux warriors. Custer knew he had no choice but to attack, although several of his junior officers tried to talk him into retreating so they could wait for the rest of the Army to catch up.

* * *

After receiving word that soldiers were nearing the village, Minikajau organized the braves into several units and sent them to strategic areas in the foothills of the valley. Little did Custer realize that he was greatly outnumbered until he was surrounded by hundreds of warriors, screaming their war cries.

* * *

While waiting for Minikajau's signal, Tanc, Brave Eagle, Little Deer and her braves circled a small group of soldiers that had been separated from the larger Army contingency.

"We will make them use up their bullets and then attack," Tanc said. "Tell the others to ride as swiftly as possible around them. Make them shoot."

Brave Eagle nodded, knowing many braves would die. Little Deer was the first to fall. Eventually, more than twenty of their warriors lay dead or wounded – but her plan worked. An eerie silence followed when both soldiers and braves no longer heard the sound of gunfire. Encouraged by their success, the Indians charged the white men, who huddled behind the dead bodies of their horses and their fellow soldiers. The battle was over and the Sioux survivors proudly displayed their trophies. Knowing that a battle was still going on elsewhere, Tanc ordered her braves away from the carnage and joined the rest of the tribe as they systematically destroyed the 7th Calvary.

* * *

Staring at the Indian encampment, Lt. Col. Custer summoned two of his most trusted scouts to make sure his soldiers outnumbered the villagers. He had learned his lesson well from his Civil War exploits. Back then, he had been more interested in victory than casualties. In the end it cost him his commission as General and he was demoted to Captain. The blow to his ego left him embittered and smarter, but no wiser. Now, he only took on battles he was assured of winning.

"How many warriors are there?" he demanded.

"Maybe a hundred. No more," Curly, his Crow scout replied. He had located the village two weeks before and watched them for the better part of a day.

"Good. We should be able to take them out without too much loss. I want the village burned afterward. These savages need to learn who is in control."

Confident that a hundred Sioux was not a match for the one thousand, well-armed soldiers under his command, Custer decided it was a waste to send out more scouts to confirm what he had just been told.

Dividing his men into three battalions, he ordered two to circle around the village so they could attack from different directions.

"We'll show them what a real army is," he threatened.

Custer waited a few hours and grew impatient. Unwilling to wait for the two battalions to get in place, he charged the village with his own group. Four thousand Indians poured from the tents. Less than six hours later, Custer and over two hundred soldiers had been killed.

* * *

Tanc watched the soldiers racing toward the village and shook her head.

"They have no respect for their ponies."

Little did she know how prophetic her words actually were. When Custer saw hundreds of braves pouring from the tents, he tried to halt the attack. Unfortunately, he was well beyond the point of no return and found himself surrounded. Ordering his bugler to sound retreat and then re-rally the troops, he summoned his senior officers for their final orders.

"Tell the men to close ranks, dismount and form a tight circle."

"Yes sir. What about the horses, sir?"

"Kill them!"

"Sir?" asked his second in command, sure he had misunderstood.

"I said kill them. We'll use their bodies as shields."

"But Colonel, sir, how will we get home?"

"The Indians have horses, Captain. Once we teach them a lesson, we'll take what we need."

"Begging your pardon, Colonel, but..."

"You have your orders, Captain. This isn't up for discussion."

Saluting, the officers departed, racing to relay their commander's orders. Reluctantly, the soldiers did as they were told. The most experienced knew it was a mistake but prayed they were wrong.

* * *

When Tanc saw the enemy circling and then dismounting, she shook her head. Some might have escaped if they had run for the river. It was the slaughtering of the horses that convinced her that these white men were crazy. Indian and horse shared a special bond. Killing them to use them as shields was unthinkable, not to mention totally illogical.

Letting out the traditional war cry, she signaled her braves to attack. The small band joined the main body of

Indians in their attack, focusing on the yellow-haired man in the center of the ring. Nudging Demon away from the circling braves, she located Brave Eagle and pointed to their target.

Nodding, he called to several braves to follow him and charged the outer line of defense. Jumping over the dead bodies, he guided his horse straight at Yellow Hair. Two soldiers tried to pull him off his horse, but he kicked them away and pointed his rifle at his target. Even amongst the other gunfire, Tanc could separate that one sound from the others. In slow motion, she saw Brave Eagle fall from his horse, clutching his side.

Kneeing Demon, Tanc gripped his sides with her legs as he sailed over the heads of the white men anxious to get to her fallen friend. Already, soldiers were beating on him with their rifles. Tanc wanted vengeance. Diving off Demon's back, she landed on the backs of several men and began fighting her way toward Brave Eagle's body. Several braves had followed her and were forcing their way forward.

Reaching her goal, Tanc pulled her knife from her scabbard, stabbed two of the soldiers and shoved them to the side. Grabbing another by the hair, she sliced his throat. When the rest realized they were being attacked from behind, they spun around and stopped. The sight of the tall, red-haired woman caught them by surprise, giving her and her fellow braves the opportunity they needed. Within seconds, the soldiers were dead.

Kneeling, Tanc ignored the fighting around her to check on her friend, expecting to find him dead. Surprisingly he wasn't, although she knew he was seriously injured. More Indians had succeeded in breaching the front line. Now Indian and soldier struggled in hand-to-hand combat. Tanc was torn between helping Brave Eagle and going after Yellow Hair. Looking around, she was just in time to see Rain In The Face complete the task.

Satisfied, Tanc leaned down to check Brave Eagle's injuries. Neither she nor her companions noticed the Crow scout lying a few feet away, pointing a gun, until they heard the blast. Immediately, he was attacked and killed.

Tanc felt as if she had been hit in the back by a club. Falling forward, she braced herself with one arm and reached around with her other hand to feel the area that was now burning like fire. A heaviness settled in her chest and she coughed. Blood spewed from her mouth, splattering over her friend's face and chest. Feeling weak and unable to support her weight, she shifted slightly to keep from falling on Brave Eagle, and then collapsed. The sounds of fighting grew faint. Tank felt cold. She was dying and she wondered how many more times Death would take her before even he grew tired of her game.

CHAPTER 16

SAIRA RELEASED that timeline and continued following the *thread* further backward. When she finally found the one intersecting Constance's, she switched strands and followed it forward until it again intersected with Sabnock. From there, she traced the historian's essence to the barrier protecting the Great Beyond. Two small golden orbs blocked her path.

"You don't belong here, Traveler," one of them said, gently.

"I'm searching for someone," Saira replied, hunting for the strand that would lead her past them.

"We don't live in your time. You won't find who you seek here."

"Maybe not, but are you so sure? There are always *threads* or remnants of them lying around. It's only a matter of time before I find what I'm looking for."

The orbs flickered as if suddenly nervous and then vanished.

Unwilling to accept defeat, Saira examined the strand she had followed. After close scrutiny, she noticed it tapered slightly when it neared the barrier until it seemed to disappear. The Traveler suspected it was an illusion. If

171

the thread ended at the barrier, it would hang loose instead of being stretched so tightly. The question now was, did she really want to see where it led? The two orbs reappeared before she had an answer.

"You can't cross over. It's forbidden."

"Forbidden by whom? I don't want to enter your world, but I must locate the owner of this *thread*. If it means breaking your rules, then so be it. I'm not bound by that which lies beyond your wall."

"You don't understand. Once you pass through the barrier, you can't return."

"So you say. It obviously isn't stopping you," Saira reasoned.

"We are the guardians. We're allowed to go where we want, when we want."

"Are you saying the others don't have a choice?"

"Of course they do. This isn't a prison. Those who come here may leave after their initial transition or they can stay of their own free will."

"Good. Then I see no reason why I can't enter, find the historian and return here with her if she wants."

One orb sighed. Saira smiled at the very human response.

"You don't belong here. The historian does. Please just go away," it pleaded.

"I will, but only if you tell her I need to see her. If she refuses to talk to me, then I'll leave."

One of the orbs disappeared and was immediately replaced by another. Saira was surprised that she could see a difference, but then realized that they were as individual as the essence they held.

"What do you want, Traveler?" the newest orb demanded.

"You are Constance?"

"I am."

"I've traveled a great distance to speak to you. Dis asked me to find you."

"Dis? The Underlord? Why?"

"Apparently he's concerned about one of his subjects. A demon named Sabnock."

The orb's light began to shimmer. Saira recognized the reaction now as agitation.

"What about her? Is she well?"

"No. She has been hunting for you. She even threatened Dis because she thought he was holding you hostage to force her to rejoin his legions."

Constance laughed.

"That's definitely Sabnock. She isn't afraid of anything, an endearing flaw in her, I have to admit."

"True, and it will lead to her destruction unless you stop her. If she discovers where you've gone, she'll find her way here."

"She can't! No one comes here unless it's their time and even then..." Constance exclaimed, but didn't sound very convincing. Although she would have chosen life in the Underworld if it meant being with Sabnock, she was in transition and not yet allowed to choose where she would spend eternity. The reasons weren't quite clear, but had something to do with the life she had led.

The Great Beyond was for those who were neither exemplary nor extremely bad. Only the Chosen were allowed entry. With great sadness, she had accepted her fate. Transitions took a long time due to the unusual adjustments the individual had to make to adapt to their new life. Occasionally one of the inhabitants would leave, but very few journeyed beyond the barriers of the Great Beyond...unless the situation was extremely dire.

"Sabnock's love for you drives her beyond reason. She's not one to give up, once she makes up her mind about something. That's what made her such a powerful leader in the Underlord's Legions."

"Along with the strength of her convictions," Constance said.

She knew she had to stop the demon from tracking her to the barrier. If she found it, she would do her best to force her way in and possibly be destroyed. The rules of the Great Beyond did not allow for exceptions.

"Take me to her."

"Now?" Saira asked, surprised.

"If you have the time."

"That's all I do have," the apparition replied. "How do we do this?"

"Hold out your hand."

Doing as she was told, Saira was surprised when the orb rested gently on her palm.

"Now, close your fingers, but don't squeeze. These vessels are delicate."

"What happens if it breaks?"

"I don't know, it's never happened before. I'm not too anxious to find out, though."

"Me neither."

The trip to the present was instantaneous.

CHAPTER 17

THE FUNERAL service was short and simple. Wrapped in a cloak provided by Yemaya, the historian's body was cradled tenderly in the demoness' arms. Several wolves paced nervously at the edge of the forest, watching for anything or anyone that didn't belong.

Yemaya stood several feet away, her arms wrapped around Dakota. The journalist sobbed quietly, her head pressed against her lover's shoulder. Regina lay next to her mistress, her attention focused on the tall demoness. The old queen had never seen a demon before and was curious about her. Like Vyushir, her wolf guardian, she lacked the normal smell and noticeable heartbeat of mortals. Still, there was a difference between the demoness and the spirit.

Ekimmu and Sarpe stood a few feet away, watching. Sabnock kneeled beside the grave and lay the body on a bed of straw and herbs. Straightening the cloak, she tucked it under Constance's chin.

"I will find you, my love," she vowed quietly, not caring who heard. Tears slid down her cheeks. Picking up one hand, she pressed it against her lips and then placed it under the cloak. Reaching down, she tucked the garment around the body as if trying to protect her deceased lover from the cold. Afterward, she stood and turned to look at the other mourners.

"Thank you."

Stepping away from the grave, the demoness passed her hand over the opening. Flames exploded from the earth and soared skyward, temporarily blinding the mortal onlookers. Only Sabnock and Sarpe were able to watch the fire consuming Constance's body, destroying all evidence of her existence.

"It iss done," Sarpe said, nodding her approval.

"Yes," Sabnock agreed sadly and walked into the forest, alone once again.

Dakota wiped her tears away, walked over to the gravesite and peered into the dark hole. Gray ashes covered the bottom. After notifying her and Yemaya of Constance's passing, Sarpe had given them a short explanation of Sabnock's relationship with the librarian. Being an ancient spirit, she kept it simple.

"Goodbye," Dakota whispered and then pulled a small bundle from her jacket pocket and dropped it inside the grave.

Yemaya cocked her head slightly, curious, but didn't ask.

"I know it's ridiculous," the journalist said, looking back at her lover for reassurance. "I wanted her to have something to take with her, so I gave her one of my pens and a small notebook. She was an historian. Stupid, huh?"

Yemaya shook her head and pulled Dakota into her arms and held her for a few moments.

"No, she would appreciate the thought."

"Yeah. I hope the pen works better for her than me," Dakota joked, trying unsuccessfully to lighten the mood.

"I wish we could do something for Sabnock," she whispered, forcing back the tears.

"I know. Maybe later. For now, though, I think she needs to be by herself."

Dakota nodded her head sadly. Separating, the two headed back to the estate.

Ekimmu and Sarpe followed a short distance behind. Neither spoke. There was nothing Sarpe could say to ease Ekimmu's loss.

* * *

Sabnock stood on the edge of the cliff looking at the river several hundred feet below. The moon glistened off the water, making it shine like a silver strand of light. If she had been mortal, the demoness would have thrown herself into the river, ending her misery.

"And we would have never met," a voice whispered.

Spinning around, Sabnock saw an apparition shimmering in the shadows a short distance away holding a small, golden orb in her palm.

"Who are you?" she demanded, angry at the intrusion.

"Just a traveler," Saira replied, walking up to her. "I've brought you someone."

Sabnock looked around suspiciously.

"Who?"

"Hold out your hand."

Confused, the demoness did as she was told. Saira placed the orb on the outstretched palm and stepped back.

"Be gentle with her. Don't squeeze," she ordered and disappeared.

* * *

Sabnock stood still, holding the object, not sure what to do.

"It was a nice funeral," a different voice said, almost causing the demoness to drop the orb.

"Constance?"

Heart pounding, she thought she was imagining things.

"Who else?"

"I hunted for you."

"I know. I thought...hoped we would meet in your world. It wasn't meant to be."

"But you're here now. Tell me how to find you and I'll join you."

"No! You can't. You must let me go, Lynara," Constance said, knowing how much those words would hurt.

"I can't. My life has no meaning now without you."

"Then give it meaning. This isn't forever. We've been apart before."

The demoness sighed. Once again she had found her one love and once again she was losing her.

"I've grown weary of my life, of this loneliness," she confessed, sadly.

"I know, my love, but true death comes only when the time is right."

"Demons don't die. They may go elsewhere but they don't die."

Constance could feel her lover's pain. It matched her own, knowing she too would have to let go once again.

"Are you happy where you are, Constance?" Sabnock asked, interrupting the librarian's thoughts.

"As happy as I could be without you."

"What's it like there?"

Constance laughed. Her voice seemed young and vibrant now, like when they had been lovers.

"Not much different than the mortal world. Maybe a little more peaceful and everyone gets along rather well, although we still have our squabbles."

"Do you still feel love or loneliness or other human emotions?"

"Human emotions? You know better than that. You're not human and yet you love me. You feel sadness and pain."

"Now I do, but when I was leading Dis' Legions, I don't remember feeling anything. I think I learned them from you."

"They were always there. You only had to find the right incentive...and yes, all of the emotions exist where I'm at, even the darker ones. Sometimes I think they are stronger than ever in the Beyond."

Sabnock was surprised. She had suspected Constance's soul had gone to the Great Beyond. It was rumored to be a place for those souls too special to go to the Overworld or the Underworld.

"But I thought..."

"That it was Paradise? Far from it. Paradise would be hell for people like me. Too homogenous. No, this place is better than the mortal world, but it's far from perfect."

"Can you touch and feel? Do people make love or hold each other?"

"Yes. What you see here is only my essence. The orb keeps it together outside the barrier."

Sabnock slowly sank to her knees. Holding the small vessel close to her face, she tried to see what Constance looked like but failed.

"What do you look like?"

"I'm just like you remember. Nothing has changed, nothing will change."

"Then you're still alone."

"No."

Surprised, Sabnock didn't know whether to be happy or hurt.

"You have someone?" she whispered, swallowing the lump in her throat.

"I have many friends there, but no, no lovers. I waited thousands of years to join you in death. I can wait a while longer."

"If I could kill myself now, I would," Sabnock declared.

"And if you did, we would never be together."

"We'll never be together. I will go on, forever the warrior. It's better you find someone else to love who will love you."

"You give up too easily, Lynara. Where is that warrior spirit now?"

"Gone, I'm afraid. I'm tired, Constance. I've spent my whole life fighting battles that weren't mine to fight, trying to be something I was never meant to be. I should have known better."

Invisible hands cupped her face as tears slid down her cheeks. To feel Constance's touch was almost as painful as not feeling it at all. Bowing her head, she cried softly, not caring anymore that true warriors never cried.

"True warriors feel pain, my love. They cry and hurt like everyone else. You've seen more death than I can ever imagine possible."

Sabnock couldn't think of anything to say. Her sorrow and loneliness were so great, she couldn't imagine going on but knew she had no choice. Straightening her shoulders, she stared into the orb and grimaced.

"Death. I've known It's touch so many times and yet never really understood the meaning. Finding you, I long for it, but know it will never really happen...and even if it did, we'd still be worlds apart. Do you think I'll ever see you again?"

"It's inevitable. Nothing can keep us apart forever. I would never allow it."

Sabnock smiled. She could almost believe it possible.

"What's a few hundred or thousand more years?" Constance continued.

"Forever," Sabnock replied, wistfully.

The historian realized there wasn't anything more she could do or say to comfort the demoness. Feeling a tug from her new world, she realized their time together was almost over.

Sabnock sensed it also and released her grip on the orb. "I guess this is it."

"For now, my love, but not forever, I promise you. When the time is right, we will be together again. It's our destiny. If you believe it is so, it will happen."

"Then I have no choice but to believe, but..."

"No! There is no 'but' between you and I, only when."

The orb shimmered brightly and then disappeared. Looking at her empty hands, Sabnock shook her head, wanting desperately to believe.

"When..." she whispered to the emptiness she was feeling inside.

CHAPTER 18

TIRED OF fighting, Sabnock accepted the medical discharge offered to her after her last tour in Afghanistan. Had she not been so depressed, she would have found it amusing to be perfectly fit while listening to the military doctor telling her she wouldn't be able to carry her backpack or pass the fitness test. After collecting her final paycheck, she disappeared. Several of her military buddies tried their best to locate her, but it was as if she had disappeared from the planet. Eventually they gave up, assuming she had either been killed somewhere or just didn't want to be found.

* * *

Fifteen years later, Sabnock found herself working for NYPD as a bomb specialist. Changing the records on her background was a simple matter for a demoness. She could always make the documents reflect whatever facts she wanted and change her appearance enough to make sure she wasn't recognized if she ever ran into anyone from her past.

Putting on her uniform, she stared blankly at the image in the mirror. As much as she wanted to, she could never bring herself to change her hair color or style. That was perhaps the one weakness in her appearance that could give her away. Still, if anyone asked, she didn't look a day over 30 and had her records to back her up. Lynara Sabnock no longer existed. She was Brandy Sabnock, no relation. Her fellow officers called her Red.

"You going to the New Year's party next week?" Sylvia asked, slamming her locker shut.

"Nah. I never liked those things. I'll probably stay home."

"You are sooo predictable. I just won fifty bucks."

"How's that?" Sabnock asked, snapping her utility belt around her waist.

"The guys bet me you'd either show up at the party or be out with some hot chick."

"You'd think they'd know better by now. They've been making that bet for the last three years."

"I love suckers who never learn. So, considering I'm going to be fifty bucks richer, you want to meet me for a few drinks after we get off? My treat."

"Sure, as long as something doesn't come up. Catch ya later."

Grabbing her hat, Sabnock strolled away, her long legs giving her a natural grace. Several officers, male and female, stopped what they were doing to watch her. Sylvia shook her head, wishing she could attract that sort of attention.

CHAPTER 1 9

THE DIVORCE had been ugly. His wife had gotten custody of the kids and alimony. Furious, he swore she'd never get a dime. In fact, if everything worked out, he'd still be able to collect on the insurance policy he was maintaining on her. Karen was going to have a very nasty accident, the victim of a terrorist bombing. Kenny just loved the thought of the Muslims getting blamed for his ex's death. He hated anyone and everyone that he didn't consider a red-blooded American.

The bomb was easier to make than he imagined, thanks to some information he had acquired from a radical militia group. They were more than willing to teach him everything he needed to know once they realized he was as *patriotic* as they were.

Three weeks at their base camp in West Virginia was enough to make him proficient at putting together small, remote-controlled bombs that could be activated by a timer or a cell phone call. Kenny had chosen the cell phone. It gave him a better opportunity to make sure Karen was in her classroom.

The school was three miles from where he lived. Everyone knew who he was so they didn't think too much about him showing up to talk to Karen. She had never told anyone about what an asshole he really was, although some suspected. Perhaps if she had, someone would have stopped and questioned him a little more, instead of taking his word that Karen had asked him to deliver some reading material she had forgotten to her classroom.

The room was empty. Everyone was at lunch. Pushing aside some supplies tucked away in a cabinet, he gently placed the bomb on the shelf and then put some papers on top of it. Shutting the door, he smirked.

Mess with me, bitch! I told you I'd get even! he thought. Walking from the room, hands in his pockets, he whistled cheerfully to himself. Several teachers gave him a strange look but didn't say anything.

Karen was having lunch with three other teachers when an aide let her know her ex-husband was on the premises.

"Damn!"

"Everything okay?" Jilly, a close friend and fellow associate, asked.

"It's Kenny. He's here."

"What the hell does that jerk want?"

"I don't know but it can't be good. Be a dear and call Frank. He was supposed to get that restraining order."

"Well, if he's like the other attorneys I know, it's still sitting on his desk, but I'll check. Want me to come along just in case?"

"No, Kenny talks a good threat but for the most part he's harmless. I just wanted the court order to keep him away from the kids and me. He can be a real pain sometimes and Sandy and Travis are scared to death of him."

"Their own father?"

"Kenny doesn't know the meaning of the word. The only reason he fought for custody was to keep from paying the child support and to piss me off."

"So why'd you ever marry the creep?"

"It's a long story. Maybe I'll tell you one day when we have time. Right now, I'd better go see what he wants."

Kenny was waiting for Karen on the school steps outside the main entrance. When she finally arrived, he tossed his lit cigarette down and stepped on it.

"About time you got here," he hissed.

"What do you want, Kenny?"

"I want to know why you got that fuckin' restraining order against me. How am I supposed to visit the kids?"

"Call me and we'll meet somewhere, with a police escort, of course."

Looking around to see if anyone was in hearing distance, he grinned when he found it was just Karen and him.

"Well, baby, I'll tell you what. You just keep pissing me off and I'll have to show you how a real man treats his woman."

"I know how a real man treats a woman. Maybe one day you'll be that real man, Kenny, but you sure as hell aren't one now. Is that the only reason you came here? Because if it is, I'm calling the police. It's about time you realized you can't always have your way."

Glaring ominously at her, Kenny decided he had better leave.

"Call them. You don't scare me and neither do they. Now shouldn't you be getting back to the kiddies before they tear up your room?"

"You know I don't have class for another hour-and-a-half. Geez, Kenny. You are so fucked up you can't even remember the easy stuff."

Turning her back on him, she walked into the building without looking back.

"Oh, I remember," he smirked. "I remember everything." Looking at his watch, he grinned. Only three more hours and the kids would be gone, leaving just Karen in the classroom. He had debated on whether to set the bomb off while they were present or wait. He had decided that waiting was a better solution. He really didn't want to be responsible for anyone else's death, just his ex-wife's. Besides, if he set the bomb off too soon, someone might connect his visit to the explosion.

After leaving Kenny, Karen went to the principal's office to tell Mr. Johnston what was going on. She had deliberately tried to keep her private life just that, but now realized it was a mistake. Stopping outside the door, she ran into the teacher Kenny had talked to just before entering the school.

"Hey, Karen, did Kenny get a hold of you? He's got those books you forgot."

"What books?" she asked, frowning.

"The ones for your assignment. I saw him about thirty minutes ago and he said you asked him to bring them."

Karen could feel her heart pounding.

"What did he do with them?"

"Oh, I saw him going into your classroom with them. I guess you missed each other. Well, gotta run. See you later."

"Shit!" she muttered under her breath, trying to think clearly. "What the hell is he up to?"

Shaking her head, she knocked on the door and heard a loud voice yell for her to come in.

"Sorry for interrupting your lunch, Mr. Johnston, but I think we may have a problem."

Quickly outlining the details of her meeting with Kenny and her conversation with her associate, she voiced her concerns about her ex-husband's actions.

"Maybe we'd better go check the room," he suggested.

Everything looked normal. Nothing was out of place or changed around since going to lunch. Pulling open her desk drawers, she shuffled the files nervously. Then she looked under and inside each student desk while the principal checked the cabinets. Relieved, she looked at the principal.

"Sorry, Mr. Johnston, maybe I'm just paranoid."

"No problem, Karen. It's better to be safe than sorry."

It was when she walked past the last cabinet near her desk that she noticed several books on the windowsill. Frowning, she tried to remember why they would be there instead of inside one of the cabinets.

"Something wrong?" he asked.

"I'm not sure." Picking up the books, she turned them over and looked at the titles. "I'm sure I kept these in the cabinet."

When she opened the door, she noticed several objects had been shifted and documents placed at odd angles. Hand shaking, she gently picked up the papers and immediately spotted a small, brown, nylon bag pushed against the back wall. Heart pounding, she inhaled and then slowly exhaled. Her hands trembled slightly as she backed slowly toward the door, trying to remain calm.

"Clear the building," she whispered, afraid that speaking in a normal tone would set the bomb off. "I think the bastard planted a bomb in here."

CHAPTER 20

SABNOCK RECEIVED the bomb call with only two hours of work left. The day had been slow and she was almost grateful for the break in boredom. Still, she wasn't looking forward to this incident, although she had to respond to it as the trained bomb specialist.

By the time she arrived at the school, everyone had been evacuated and the building was surrounded by policemen, firemen, paramedics and the press. Sabnock hated the press. They were the one group that could cause her some heartburn if her picture ever appeared in a newspaper or magazine.

Making sure her hat was pulled low over her forehead and her sunglasses firmly in place, she pushed through the crowd, keeping her head down. As she neared the police barricade, she heard someone call out to her.

"Sabnock? Hey, Sabnock, is that you?"

Looking around, she spotted a man in his early forties, shoving his way toward her carrying a camera. A woman was following close behind, trying to avoid the bodies being pushed around.

"Sabby, we hunted all over for you," he exclaimed, smiling brightly.

"I'm sorry, do I know you?" she asked, instantly recognizing Squirrel from her time in Afghanistan.

"It's me, Squirrel," he said, patting her on the back.

Taking off her sunglasses, she stared blankly at him.

"Do I know you?"

Squirrel stepped back and bumped into his companion. Confused, he shook his head as if trying to clear is mind. His Sabnock had green eyes. This woman had blue eyes and was no more than thirty.

"Gosh, officer, I thought you were someone I knew a long time ago."

Glancing at her name tag, he frowned.

"You don't by chance have an older sister or cousin do you?"

"Not that I know of. Why?"

"Well, it's just that you look so much like Sabby and she had the same last name as you...not to mention red hair. If you were about fourteen or fifteen years older, I'd swear you were her."

"Look, I'm sorry I'm not this Sabby person, but I have a job to do. Good luck in finding her."

Sabnock turned and stepped past several police officers, leaving Squirrel behind. Renewing old acquaintances was impossible. There'd be too many questions and no good answers.

"She wasn't the Sabby you were looking for?" his companion asked, tugging on his arm to get his attention.

"No," he replied sadly. "I wish she had been. The guys owed her a lot."

"Well, maybe one day you'll find her. Right now, though, we have a story to do. The boss expects us to take some good pictures for the six o'clock news."

Squirrel nodded. Now wasn't the time for nostalgia.

"Where's the bomb?" Sabnock asked the cop at the school entrance.

"Inside. Mac will show you. Your gear is already there, too."

"Thanks."

Other than Mac, the school was empty. Her bomb suit was sitting outside the classroom door, along with a helmet with a ballistic shield, special gloves and a built in cooling system. Putting on each section, she strapped everything as tight as she could, making sure there was little chance of something coming loose.

After everything was secured, she told Mac to take off. If the bomb exploded before she could disarm it, the chances were the suit wouldn't keep her from being injured. If the explosives were powerful enough, it could even kill her.

Sabnock shuffled into the room and walked to the cabinet. The brown bag looked harmless enough but she wasn't fooled. Because of its size, there was a good chance it contained C4, a plastic explosive that was so powerful, a small amount could destroy several rooms.

Taking her time, she examined as many sides of the bag as possible. No wires or switches were visible. She hoped that meant the bottom was clear also. If it contained a pressure switch, the moment she moved the bag the bomb would be activated. Had the bomber placed the package on a lower shelf she would have called in the bomb-bot to remove it.

Placing the bag she had brought into the room with her on the desk, Sabnock slowly unzipped it and pulled out a large, flat, spatula-looking device. Hopefully, she could slip it under the package without activating any pressure switches. Carefully, she slid it under the bag, making sure her movements were slow and precise. Whenever she felt it hit something, she held her breath and stopped, waiting and listening. When nothing happened, she inched it a little further.

Sabnock knew she could use her powers to examine the contents but refused the temptation. Where was the challenge if she didn't play by the rules she had established long ago. She didn't just want to play human, she wanted to feel what they felt or at least as close to it as possible.

Today was the first time she had ever broken into a legitimate sweat, not the phony ones she had faked to keep others from being suspicious when she was in stressful situations. Even her heart pounded so loudly she could hear it beating.

So this is what it feels like. This is the fear they have to live with.

The thought was overwhelming. Sabnock had spent thousands of years hoping to experience almost all that was human. Her greatest achievement had been love. It was also her greatest loss. There had been moments of sadness, longing, joy, regret and many other emotions but never fear – until now. Why now?

The answer eluded her, but the fear was real.

Sabnock felt her hands trembling and she released the grip on the slidebar. Looking curiously at her sweaty palms, she rubbed them together and then dried them on a rag. A voice from outside the classroom door distracted her.

"Sabnock, you okay?"

"Mac, get the hell out of here!" she yelled. "And you pull this trick again, I'll have you transferred to meter maid. Didn't anyone warn you not to sneak up on someone trying to deactivate a bomb?"

"Sorry. It was taking so long, I thought you might need something."

"No, but thanks. Now leave. It'll probably be another thirty minutes before I decide what to do with this thing."

"Okay. Good luck!"

Turning her attention back to the bomb, she grabbed the handle and continued pressing it under the bag. The sound of something clicking made her jump.

CHAPTER 2 1

KENNY STOOD among the crowd, listening and waiting. Not sure what to do, he realized his attempts to kill his ex had been ruined. Now he needed to figure out what to do with the bomb. If the FBI got ahold of the components, it was possible they could be traced to the militants – and from there to him.

Nervously fingering the cell phone in his pocket, he pushed his way through the crowd and moved to stand by a building further away but with a better view. Several times he pulled the cell phone out and dialed the number but then closed the cover before pushing the enter button. Hopefully, the bomb expert would screw up and detonate it. It would solve all of his problems. Better a policeman get killed than he go to prison.

When someone yelled, he looked up to see what had happened. Near the front steps of the school stood the officer holding the bomb. Watching her moving slowly toward the steps, he realized he had no choice. Quickly dialing the number, he glanced back at the policeman and then down at the phone. With his finger poised over the send button, he hesitated.

Sabnock felt every muscle in her body aching from the stress of carrying the bomb, not to mention the weight and awkwardness of the suit. She had almost reached the first step when she heard a cell phone ring. The sound of the explosion was deafening but the power behind it surprised her even more. The demoness felt herself being hurled through the air and slammed against the brick wall of the school.

Unimaginable pain screamed through every nerve in her body. Barely able to open her eyes, she saw several people bending over her, some frantically trying to remove her bomb suit. Mac was talking to her but she couldn't hear him. She could tell he was screaming, trying to tell her to hang on.

* * *

Karen was stunned by how loud the explosion was. Had any of her kids been in the room with her or the rooms around hers when it blew, all of them would have been killed or seriously injured. Now, a brave officer was at the very best seriously injured and perhaps even dying. Glancing around the crowd, she knew Kenny had to be nearby. The timing was too perfect.

It took her several minutes to locate him. When she did, she saw he was looking at her angrily. Calling to a policeman, she quickly pointed him out as he was walking rapidly away from the scene. The officer radioed the dispatcher, giving her a description of the man and what he was wearing. Within minutes, several undercover and uniformed cops were in hot pursuit, guns drawn.

Minutes later, three gunshots were heard. The crowd looked around, trying to see what was happening but unable to locate the source. Shrugging, they turned their attention back to the paramedics and the officers working to save their comrade.

Sabnock knew she was dying. She could feel the coldness creeping up her arms and legs. The pain slowly subsided, leaving her lethargic.

"Hang on!" a voice yelled, breaking through the deafening silence. Focusing on the voice, she blinked several times trying to clear away the fog. Mac's face was only inches from hers, his eyes pleading for her to fight.

How many more times am I going to go through this?

"So, we meet again," the voice said. "How many more times do you want to?"

"I don't," Sabnock sighed. "I'm tired of these games. I'm tired of living."

"You would give up so much for eternal darkness?" Death asked.

"Yes."

"You understand that, as a demon, you can never return to the Underworld if you take this path?"

"If that is my fate, I accept it," Sabnock said wearily. She no longer cared.

"And Constance? You would give up your chance to be reunited? You would break your promise to her?"

Sabnock hesitated.

"Why did you have to mention her?" she cried out in anguish. "She will be better off without me. Maybe now she will find someone else."

"In all the years of her existence, you were her only love. Now, she knows you still live. She believes you will be reunited one day. Are you willing to destroy that belief...that chance? Is your love so weak you would condemn her to an eternity of loneliness?"

"Never!"

"Choose then, demoness. Do you accept life or the final darkness?" Sabnock had known all along that this would happen. Death had always given her the choice and she had repeatedly lacked the courage to make it final. "It doesn't take courage to die when life has grown unbearable," Death whispered. "Courage comes from choosing pain over the freedom I offer."

"You've never mentioned Constance before. Why now?"

Death smiled. "Because you've never made the wrong decision before."

Gathering her strength, she invited the darkness in, wondering what would happen next.

* * *

Dis was furious. One of his most valuable demons was missing. He had felt it the moment her essence had disappeared and knew she was gone forever.

"Where is she?" he demanded of the shrouded figure standing in front of him.

"She is where she belongs," it answered, not in the least intimidated by the Underlord's behavior.

"Sabnock was one of my best commanders. I may have need of her."

"Then you will have to do without her. She is no longer yours."

"How dare you take what isn't yours!" Dis roared, banging his fist on the table.

Death laughed and then turned to stare at a spot to his right.

"It would seem you have a guest," It said.

Rolling his eyes, the Underlord knew immediately about whom he was talking.

"I thought we had an agreement," he bellowed.

Saira laughed.

"I said I would try, but this tug was too strong and came too quickly for me to give you a warning. I have never met Death before."

"Pray that you never do again," Dis replied, turning back to his first guest. "In case you don't know her, this is Saira. She is a traveler."

"It's a pleasure to meet you, Saira. I've known about you for a long time."

"Then we have something in common," she replied smiling. "And you have lost Sabnock," she said to Dis.

"Lost? Stolen, you mean. She should have been returned to me, but Death decided to interfere in my business."

"You are growing old, my friend. Have you forgotten? Sabnock was freed by you a long time ago. You no longer had a claim on her."

"Her freedom was revocable at any time. She was mine to command."

"No, she wasn't."

Saira listened to the two entities arguing. They were two of the most powerful beings in existence and this was perhaps the only time she would ever see them together, particularly as Death was so elusive.

"Couldn't you have waited?" Dis asked. "Trouble is brewing and I need her to command my legions. Bring her back!"

"I am many things, Dis, but a magician I'm not. Sabnock is beyond my reach now. She chose her fate and has fulfilled her destiny. Besides, even if I could, I wouldn't. I have a great fondness for her and she's earned her reward."

Saira stared at Death, surprised that It had just lied to the Underlord. When the shrouded figure turned to look at her, she had the impression It was smiling.

Dropping into his chair, Dis uttered a few curse words and then sighed.

"I suppose you're right."

"I'm always right, but thank you. It's not often you admit to being wrong."

"I didn't say that," he growled. "I said you were right. Obviously, I had no say in the matter."

Smirking, Death had to agree, although it did seem to be a technicality.

"Well, I really must go. The mortal world keeps me quite busy these days. Oh, by the way. You might take a particular interest in the newest addition to your coffers."

"Why? I have demons and minions for that. I have guests waiting for me."

"Hmmm. Perhaps I was mistaken. I thought for sure you'd like to meet the human who killed Sabnock. Oh well...."

"Wait!" Dis ordered jumping to his feet. "Tell me his name."

"Kenny Rothman."

"It seems my guests will have to wait a while longer. I very much want to meet this soul. He deserves a special welcome."

Death knew what such a welcome would be, but felt little compassion for the soul. It deserved everything the Underlord had planned.

Bidding Dis farewell, the dark figure disappeared. Dis rubbed his hands together, anxious to visit Soulkeeper.

"Well, this has been interesting," the apparition said, enjoying the demon's frustration. "I suppose I should leave you to your business."

"At last! And would you give me war..."

Before he could finish Saira had vanished.

"Females!" he growled. "Males are so much easier to deal with."

Calling to his minions, he strolled from the room, his shiny hooves clicking on the polished floor. Already, he was thinking about what he would do with Kenny Rothman.

CHAPTER 2 2

SAIRA HAD returned to the mortal world but was confused. For the first time in her existence, she felt no tugs. It was as if time had momentarily stopped.

"It will last but a moment," the voice promised.

"Why are you here? Is it my time now?" she asked, surprised by Death's appearance.

"That isn't for me to say. I came to answer your question."

"Question? Oh, of course. Why did you lie to Dis? You could retrieve Sabnock."

"To what purpose? Besides, now that she's with her lover, I suspect it would be the death of me to try and separate those two."

Saira snickered at the pun.

"Well, we wouldn't want that, now would we?" she teased.

"No. I took a vacation once and it created so many problems, I swore never again."

"What happened?"

"Ah, now that's another story. It'll have to wait until another time. Like you, I feel the tugs pulling on me. Our work is very different, but our lives follow a similar path. Until we meet again, Saira. Travel safely."

Before she could answer, Death was gone and the tugs began anew.

EPILOGUE

The Messenger

THE DEATH of Constance saddened Dakota. Although they had spent only a short time together, Dakota felt a strong connection to the historian. Standing on the balcony, she watched several bats diving at invisible bugs and wondered about the strange events over the past few days.

"She was special," she said, turning to look at the woman standing next to her. "I wish I could have talked to her again. She had such an amazing life." Yemaya rested her head against the top of Dakota's.

"I would have liked to have spent some time with her too. I think her death is a great loss to humanity as well as to those who knew her," Yemaya said. Taking Dakota into her arms, she stared over her lover's shoulder into the moonlit darkness.

"Do you think Sabnock is really a demoness?" Dakota asked, leaning back slightly to look at Yemaya. "I mean, she must be. How else could she have cremated Constance's body so quickly? That wasn't a trick."

"No, the flames were real. I could feel the heat..." Yemaya hesitated. It was unlike her. "It should have been hotter. It takes a lot of heat and time to completely cremate a body. Hers was gone in a matter of seconds. I have no idea how that could be done under normal circumstances."

"Well, if you can't figure it out, no one can," Dakota teased. "You have to admit, things certainly have gotten interesting since we met. I've always believed in spirits but nothing comes close to these real life experiences."

Yemaya laughed.

"I cannot argue with that."

For several minutes, Yemaya and Dakota said nothing, both enjoying the stillness of the night and each other's warm embrace. Occasionally an owl's screech could be heard in the distance. Suddenly, a wolf howled, followed by several more nearby. Iridescent silver eyes glowed at the edge of the forest.

"They're restless," Dakota said. "Do you think something is wrong?"

Yemaya shook her head.

"No. That is Regina and Voinic over there," Yemaya said, pointing slightly to the left. "Simtire is there." She moved her hand in another direction. "She brought a young male from one of the mountain packs."

"How can you see them that well? I can barely make out their shapes."

Shrugging, Yemaya ruffled Dakota's hair.

"I have good vision."

"You have great vision, you mean." Dakota frowned. "Has Simtire chosen him as her mate?"

"No. He is just a playmate. Are you worried she will forget you?"

"A little, I guess. Selfish, huh?"

"Not really. There is nothing to worry about, though. You are her mistress. She will never forget you. Wolves are very loyal."

Feeling relieved, Dakota's thoughts returned to Constance and Sabnock.

"I wonder if we'll ever see Sabnock again. I have so many questions. I mean, if she really is a demoness, then there's a chance we might see Constance again...or at least her spirit. You know, like Grandma Dakota." Dakota grew excited at the thought. "Do you think Constance might be in the spirit world? Maybe I could ask Gram."

"I really do not know, Dakota. You certainly can ask, but I sensed a great sorrow in Sabnock. It was as if she were saying a final farewell to Constance. If she is a demoness, I would think she would be able to reunite with Constance even after death if it were possible. There should have been no sadness."

Dakota couldn't deny the logic in Yemaya's words. Spirits and demons could enter the mortal world at will even if their own realms were impenetrable. Eyes tearing, she buried her face in Yemaya's chest and cried.

"I...I wouldn't...know..." she sobbed. "If you...died...I'd..."

"Shhh," Yemaya murmured, wrapping her arms around her lover. "It will never happen. I would find you wherever you were. We are one...besides, we have a lot of powerful people on our side. Who would want to take on Mari or Grandma Dakota? Now, how about we get some rest. It has been a long couple of days."

Leading Dakota back into the bedroom, she helped her undress and get into the bed. Then she slipped in next to her and pulled her lover firmly against her. Almost immediately they fell asleep.

* * *

Gaapa grinned as she watched the human writhing on the ground near the school. It was especially pleasing to know he was suffering and would continue to do so for several more minutes. Hopefully Death would take his time with Sabnock and this human would have to endure the agonizing pain awhile longer.

Standing over the body, she leaned forward and grabbed his face. Clawed fingers wrapped around his chin as she jerked his head toward her. The man's eyes widened with fear. He stared horrified at the crimson red face with the ghoulish grin. Uneven pointed teeth gleamed brightly between thin, dark brown lips. The eyes were shiny black with bright, dancing orange flames as pupils. That alone would have been terrifying, but the lumpy, wrinkled skin was covered with festering sores, reminding him of a monster he had seen in an old horror movie.

"Yessss," Gaapa said, pleased at the terror reflected in the human's eyes. "It's good to be afraid. I am just the beginning of your nightmare."

"Who...who...are...you?" he asked and realized he hadn't spoken the words aloud. The pain in his chest was unbearable; the thing before him unimaginable.

If I could just wake up, he thought. *This is only a nightmare. It has to be a nightmare.*

"*You will never sleep,*" Gaapa promised, "*and your nightmare is just beginning. The pain you feel now is nothing compared to the pain that awaits you. We have a special place for you, Kenny.*"

Amused at his confused look, Gaapa straightened up and stepped backward, passing through one of the policemen who had just holstered his gun. She laughed when the officer shivered. Mortals were so weak.

"You okay"?" the second policeman asked, looking at his partner.

"I've never shot anyone before. Is...is he dead?"

"I don't know. Let's hope so, because I don't want this bastard getting off on some insanity defense. I'd make sure of it if there weren't so many people nearby."

"You aren't very popular, are you? Not to worry. Where you're going, that will change. You'll have more attention than you can stand."

"I...don't...understand. Who...are you? Am I...dying?"

"Of course. Enjoy the moment."

"Enjoy dying? I'm...in pain. I...can't breathe."

Kenny gasped and then coughed as blood bubbled from his mouth.

"Yes. Isn't it wonderful? Only now do you understand real pain...or think you do. This is nothing compared to what you will be feeling after you are dead."

Gaapa again turned to look at Sabnock and the shrouded figure standing next to her shattered body. She had no doubt the demoness would reappear in another human form somewhere else. Sabnock had abandoned the Underworld, preferring to live as a mortal. Dying was just a formality for her. Still, Gaapa didn't take kindly to those who killed her friends. Sabnock had been the commander of Dis' many Legions and Gaapa was one of her most trusted lieutenants.

Soon my friend, she thought. *You will be moving on to your next life and I will be transporting this creature to his final destiny. I will make sure he pays for what he has put you through.*

Gaapa knew that Sabnock was in pain...great pain. Demons were not immune to physical sensations. In fact, feelings such as pleasure and pain were more heightened than in mortals.

"*Death comes,*" Gaapa said, looking down at Kenny. "*Too bad. You haven't suffered enough for what you've done. Still...*" Gaapa shrugged. "*There will be plenty of time to make up for what is lost here.*"

"*Are you done with him?*" Death asked, ignoring the body lying on the ground.

"*Yes,*" Gaapa replied. "*Sabnock, has she moved on?*"

"*She is where she wants to be,*" Death said, It's voice calm and emotionless.

"*Good. It'll be interesting to see what she does next. I almost envy her and her lives.*"

Death said nothing.

"*I guess I've prolonged his agony enough. Give me the soul,*" Gaapa said. "*I'm curious to see who Dis gives it to first.*"

"*As you wish,*" Death replied and touched Kenny's forehead. The death rattle of failing lungs filled the air. Kenny's body jerked twice and then relaxed.

"Hey, I think he just croaked," a policeman said, kneeling next to the still body.

"Great, it'll save the taxpayers a lot of money," the second replied and nudged Kenny with his foot. He wanted desperately to kick the asshole but knew better. Only seconds earlier, a fellow officer had told him that the bomb squad specialist had died.

"*Good journey to you, Gaapa,*" Death said and disappeared.

Clinching her hand tightly around the shriveled, black, walnut-sized orb she had captured leaving the

209

human's body, Gaapa cackled gleefully and vanished. She would be sure to tell Sabnock who had first rights to this soul.

* * *

Gaapa waited patiently for Dis to appear. As the Transporter of Souls, she had been in this position too many times to feel impatience. Normally, her Master didn't get involved in such things, but the soul of the human Kenny was of special interest to him. The Lord of the Underworld had little tolerance for those who harmed his followers, especially mortals.

Strolling naked from his bedroom, Dis motioned for Gaapa to come forward.

"Have you brought it?" he demanded, his anger barely under control.

"Yes, my Lord." Gaapa opened her hand and held out the last remnants of Kevin's existence. "What do you wish me to do with it?"

"Give it to me," he ordered. Gaapa placed it in his outstretched hand. The soul looked like a small pea compared to the size of Dis' palm. Raising it to eye level, he peered at the insignificant thing. "You dare to harm one of mine. She was one of my greatest commanders and you destroyed her."

Stunned at the words, Gaapa looked from the soul to the Underlord.

"I don't understand."

Dis glared at the Transporter of Souls and then softened his gaze. She and her mate, Gaap, had been by his side from almost the beginning. Gaapa was one of his most loyal servants.

210

"Sabnock is missing. She is nowhere to be found."

"But...that's impossible. Humans don't have the power to destroy us...especially one so puny as this."

"I agree. Nevertheless, Sabnock has disappeared. My servants have looked everywhere for her."

"Wouldn't Death know if she was dead? Surely..."

"Death evades the issue. I never have been able to get direct answers from Death."

"It must be very frustrating, My Lord. Such insolence should not be tolerated," Gaapa replied.

"Even I have no control over It. Death is It's own master and answers only to Itself."

Dis clenched his hand, tempted to destroy the essence of the soul. Only his desire for revenge stayed the impulse. Tossing it back to Gaapa, he turned abruptly and strolled toward the bedroom.

"Take that to the Chamber of Pain. I'll personally handle the punishment."

Bowing, Gaapa left. It was good to see her Master take an interest in something besides orgies. He had been absent too long from the Chamber.

* * *

Soneillon greeted Gaapa in his usual dour mood. As the Keeper of the Chamber of Pain, Gaapa thought the demon fitted his position well. He hated everything and everyone.

Except his job, she thought. *He's going to be unhappy that Dis will be taking away the pleasure of punishing this thing.*

"Greetings, Soneillon," she called out. "Dis wants you to take charge of this."

211

Soneillon flicked his hand in the direction of a large bowl.

"Put it with them. I'll get to it after I'm done with this one," he said.

Walking up to the demon, she peered over his shoulder at the soul lying on the table in front of him.

"What are you doing to this one?" she asked.

"He was a stalker and serial killer. Now, it is he who is stalked by his victims. At the moment they are dismembering him, joint by joint. When they are done, I will put him together and start over. The next time they'll remove his skin, piece by piece, and after that, disembowel him. Every stroke of the knife is slow and precise, intensifying his pain a thousand times."

Gaapa grinned. It was a just punishment. She knew once Soneillon had determined the proper punishment, it would get worse each time the cycle restarted. Only Dis had the power to stop him. Still, the Keeper's imagination was nothing compared to the Underlord's.

"What has this one done?" Soneillon asked, glancing toward the shriveled soul. It was unusual for one to arrive in such poor condition.

"The human killed Sabnock."

Soneillon stopped playing with the wretched soul on the table and turned to Gaapa. His normally neutral expression disappeared, replaced by unimaginable hatred. Eyes flashing, the demon made a move toward the soul. Gaapa grabbed his arm.

"Dis claimed it."

"Dis? Dis never gets involved in the punishments anymore."

"Dis claimed it," Gaapa repeated. "You will need to guard it from the others. Many will want to avenge Sabnock."

"This makes no sense. How can a mortal kill a demon? You must have misunderstood Dis."

"I didn't. Sabnock cannot be found anywhere and Death won't tell Dis anything. We have to assume she has been destroyed."

"And you say I have to protect this...this thing? I can make it pay a terrible price for what it has done...something deserving...something...*special.*"

"It's not yours to punish. Maybe when Dis grows tired of his pleasure, he'll give it to you. For now, just guard it."

"As you say," Soneillon said, shrugging.

Too easy, Gaapa thought. *You're not fooling me.*

"I warn you, Soneillon. Protect that soul or it will be you who Dis takes pleasure in. He will have no compunction in taking his wrath out on you. I seriously doubt you want to give up your position here for a few moments of gratification."

"I *said* I would guard it," Doneillon hissed. "Now, leave me. I have work to do." Turning his back on the demoness, he returned to the stalker's soul and began prodding it. Gaapa knew she had been dismissed but had no doubt the Keeper would do his job. His hatred was formidable but he wasn't stupid.

I must talk to Gaap, Gaapa thought. She hoped he wasn't away transporting souls.

* * *

"What yah be wantin', child?" Maopa asked her great-great-grandchild.

213

"Granny! Oh, Granny, it's good to see you," Dakota said, happily, aware she was now in the Spirit World. "How are you? How's Mari? And Sarpe?"

"Slow down thar a bit, youngin'. Everyone be fine. Mari's gawn visitin' Gaia...and Sarpe be with Ekimmu...makin' whoopee, I imagines. Now, why yah be a botherin' me when yah has that good lookin' woman snugglin' next to yah?"

Dakota looked at the waterfall across the lake. A mist rose from the cascading water, creating a rainbow. White birds circled above it, diving and climbing with the winds created by the thundering falls.

"It's Constance. She's dead."

"I know. I done felt her essence pass on. She were a good woman."

A tear rolled down Dakota's cheek.

"I'll miss her."

"Many will darlin', but that be the way of thangs. It be life, chile. Is that what ya came ta tells me?"

"No. I was hoping she made it to the Spirit World. Did she?" Dakota asked hopefully.

Maopa shook her head sadly.

"She ain't here...and I don't thank she be with the Twin either. She be way too good fer that un."

Dakota laughed.

"I thought that was where the good people went."

"That be where boringly good people be a-goin'. Constance weren't *that* good."

"Then where is she?"

"I don't be a-knowin' that. Have ya asked Lilith? Maybe she's with her kin."

"The Underworld?" Dakota shook her head. "I can't believe Constance would go there."

Maopa patted her granddaughter's hand.

"It ain't jest for bad people."

"I know." Dakota thought about Sabnock. "I was just hoping...a demoness named Sabnock brought Constance's body to the funeral and cremated it. I think they were in love."

"There ya go then. They be together now."

"I don't think so. Sabnock was too sad. She should have been happy if they were going to be together."

Maopa frowned.

"True 'nough. I tells ya what. Rest here fer awhile and I'll sees if'n' I kin contact Lilith. She might be a knowin' somethin' 'bout it."

"Thanks, Granny."

Settling onto the grass, Dakota closed her eyes and dreamed of Yemaya.

* * *

The nightclub was closed. Lilith had given Agra and Kali the rest of the night off. Even demonesses needed down time. Closing the ledger, she leaned back in her chair and waited. The air near her desk shimmered.

"Good evening, Maopa," Lilith said, sensing the intruder's identity.

"And ta ya too, Lilith," Maopa said, appearing suddenly. "Has ya a moment or two ta jaw a bit?"

"For you, always. What do you need?"

"It's Dakota. She be worried 'bout Constance."

"I felt her passing," Lilith said. "She was an interesting woman."

"That be so. Seems a demoness named Sabnock were at the fun'ral."

Startled, Lilith stood up and walked around the desk.

"Sabnock? I haven't thought about her in eons. She left the Underworld shortly after the Great Battle. I wonder what she has to do with Constance?"

"I was hopin' yah'd tell *me*."

"I don't know. Wait here! Maybe Dis will know."

Lilith disappeared.

"Now that be an exit," Maopa said.

* * *

Lying amongst the writhing bodies, Dis was in his glory. Minions, demons and a few privileged mortals were enjoying cunnilingus, fornication and every unimaginable debauchery. At the moment, two demons were massaging the massive erection of the Underlord. Head back, eyes shut, Dis grunted with pleasure.

"I see things haven't changed," a husky voice commented, breaking into his euphoria.

"Lilly!" Dis exclaimed, opening his eyes, pleased to see his ex. Motioning to his erection, he grinned. "You look as beautiful as ever. Care to join me?"

"It looks like you are in good hands," Lilith replied. "What can you tell me about Sabnock?"

Dis grimaced.

"You know how to ruin a party." Pushing the bodies aside, he sat up and then climbed out of the huge bed. Grabbing his robe, he slipped it on and motioned for Lilith to follow him. "She's disappeared."

"Disappeared?"

"Yes. I think Death had something to do with it, but It won't tell me anything."

"Death? What happened?"

216

"A mortal killed Sabnock. I know," he said holding up his hand. "This time it's different. She never reappeared and Death isn't talking. Arrogant bastard."

"It still gets to you, doesn't it?" Lilith asked.

"What?"

"The fact you can't control It. Death isn't a demon."

"This isn't about that. If Death knows something, It should tell me. Sabnock is one of mine. I have a right to know."

"Well, knowing you, you probably tried to order Death to tell you. Both of you are stubborn."

The deeper red blush creeping into Dis' already red cheeks gave Lilith her answer.

"I thought so."

"I am the Underlord. I don't ask...I tell," Dis stated, straightening his massive body, hoping to intimidate Lilith.

"And you see how well that worked," Lilith said, unimpressed. "Any ideas?"

"I think Saira knows something but she's off on one of her trips. Damn woman pops in uninvited, but won't show up when I summon her. You females are a royal pain."

"Someone has to keep you straight. If you find out anything will you let me know?" Lilith asked.

"Why are you interested in Sabnock now? You two were never close."

"I'm helping a friend. Sabnock may know something about the human Constance's soul. It seems that, too, is missing."

"You're doing this for a human? You're getting soft, Lilly," Dis teased.

Looking at the massive organ hanging limply but visible through the opened front of the robe, Lilith smirked.

"Apparently, so are you."

Dis's eyes widened and then his deep laughter bellowed through the Underworld. He loved battling wits with Lilith. When Lilith vanished, he shook his head and returned to the bedroom. Already his penis was swollen in anticipation of the things to come.

* * *

"He knows nothing," Lilith said to Maopa. "Sabnock has disappeared too."

"If ya hears somethin' would ya let me know?"

"Of course," Lilith replied. "I'll keep checking around."

"Thank ya."

Maopa vanished.

"Nice exit," Lilith commented.

* * *

"Wake up, Child," Maopa said, gently shaking Dakota's shoulder. "Lilith don't know nothin' but she'll let us know if'n she hears somethin'. It be time for ya to go home."

Yawning, Dakota thanked her Granny and then fell back to sleep.

* * *

Something was tickling her ear. Swatting at the irritant, Dakota turned onto her side and hugged her pillow. Fingers trailed up and down her back. Dakota shivered. When warm lips caressed her ear she smiled.

"It is about time you woke up, sleepyhead," a husky voice whispered.

Dakota swallowed. Already she could feel herself growing moist. Rolling on her back, she grabbed Yemaya by the head and leaned upward, capturing her lips. Tongues tentatively played with each other as their hands explored each other's body. Breaking the kiss, Dakota gasped for air.

"You certainly know how to wake a girl up," she said.

"Only one," Yemaya replied, leaning forward to take a nipple between her lips. Teeth playfully nipped at the left breast before moving to the right one. "You taste good." Running her hand down Dakota's stomach, Yemaya inhaled deeply. "You smell good, too, warm and musky."

"Musky! I'm not sure I like..." A finger twirled through curly blonde hair made her gasp. "Oh God," she moaned, anticipating what was to come.

Yemaya knew every inch of Dakota's body and began a slow assault on the most sensitive spots. Lips caressed her breasts, then her stomach and then moved to the inner thighs. Fingertips circled the nipples, while her thumb rubbed the aroused nub.

Dakota's skin grew pebbly with goosebumps.

"I...uhhh...I..."

"Shhhh," Yemaya murmured against Dakota's stomach just below the navel. "Just enjoy."

Not needing to be told twice, Dakota relaxed and let Yemaya perform her magic. As Yemaya's tongue explored moist, warm skin, Dakota's legs quivered. She wanted to scream so badly but wasn't quite ready. Her body felt as if it would explode when a thumb stroked the soft skin next to her clit. Like a small vibrator it moved rapidly back and forth, massaging the sensitive nerves.

"Geez!" Dakota groaned and squirmed under the persistent assault against her clit. Yemaya moved upward, as her fingers and thumb increased their pressure and speed. Taking Dakota's right nipple between her lips, Yemaya sucked gently, bringing Dakota to the brink of an orgasm...and then Yemaya stopped everything.

"What the..." Dakota exclaimed. Yemaya grinned.

"I decided to slow it down a bit," she explained.

"Slow down? Slooww down?" Dakota stammered. Before she could say anything, Yemaya started over again.

* * *

"That wasn't very nice," Dakota said.

Raising one eyebrow, Yemaya gave her a haughty look.

"Are you complaining?" she asked.

"No. I'm just saying I was sooo ready and then you stopped."

"Of course. I wanted to prolong your pleasure. Was I mistaken?" Yemaya asked, cocking her head slightly as she stared into Dakota's green eyes.

"Never! I loved every minute of it, but can I help it if you do such a good job making love?"

"No, and neither can I," Yemaya replied, grinning.

"My, aren't you sure of yourself," Dakota teased.

"Yes. Now, how about some breakfast. I am hungry."

"Again? Haven't you eaten enough?"

"Never enough when it comes to you, but I am talking people food." Poking Dakota in the ribs, Yemaya jumped out of bed and headed for the bathroom. "Would you like to share the shower?"

Dakota didn't need to be asked a second time.

* * *

The domov was empty, Gaapa was disappointed that her mate was away. He may have heard rumors about Sabnock. Gaap liked to talk a lot, but he was also a good listener. Few things got past him.

Her next choice for information was Nergal. He commanded Dis' secret police and had spies everywhere. Like Gaapa he was part of the Elite, respected and feared by most of the minions and demons of the lower orders. Fortunately, he was subordinate to her so *requesting* his presence wasn't a problem. Within minutes he was standing before her.

"You wish to see me, Gaapa," Nergal said, bowing respectfully. Gaapa wasn't fooled. Nergal resented anyone higher in rank than him, but dared not show it. Although his position was secure as an Elite, it wasn't as a commander.

"Yes. Thank you for your prompt response, Nergal." *As if you had a choice,* Gaapa thought, enjoying the game. Seniority had its privileges but superiority was more fun. Gaapa had no doubt she was superior. "Dis just told me Sabnock is missing. What do you know about this?"

A slight narrowing of Nergal's eyes was the only indication of his surprise.

"Dis told you this? I wasn't aware that Sabnock had disappeared. Why wasn't I informed immediately?" he demanded.

"That is for Dis to say. Obviously your agents are getting lax. You may go now, but you will tell me if you learn anything."

There was nothing Nergal could say or do but leave. He prided himself on his information gathering skills. That he knew nothing of Sabnock's disappearance was humiliating. His ego would drive him to find answers more than anything else she could have done. The dismissal was merely icing.

What now? Where can you be?, Gaapa wondered. *Death! Maybe It will tell me. I should have asked It when I was attending the human.*

Replaying the image of Death standing next to Sabnock when she had been killed, Gaapa swore.

I should have known something was wrong. Death took too long with you. It has never taken that long for you to move on. Gaapa had been present during most of Sabnock's passings. Rarely did the demoness die alone. Such was the life of a warrior. *What did the two of you talk about?*

"Death, I respectfully request your presence," she called out.

Instantly, It appeared in front of her.

"What can I do for you, Gaapa?" Death asked quietly.

"I seek information about Sabnock. She's missing. Dis told me you refused to answer his questions."

"His demands," It corrected. "I am not his to command."

Gaapa laughed. She could imagine the Underlord's frustration dealing with an equal...more than an equal. Death had unlimited power over demons as well as mortals.

"He knows that. It's just hard for him to accept."

Death said nothing.

"Will you tell me where she is?"

"Why do you think I know this?"

"You are Death. You know everything that happens to souls."

A slight nod confirmed her comment.

"Perhaps. If it is so, however, why would I tell you that which I would not your master?"

It was a good question. Gaapa thought about it for a few seconds.

"Courtesy," she replied.

"Courtesy?" Death seemed amused. "It is not the answer I expected. Explain."

"You and I share similar existences. You free the souls from their bodies. I transport many of them to their final destination. Our work is equally important and mutually beneficial, although it is you who wields the greatest power."

"True, but that isn't reason enough to break the trust of Sabnock."

"I would never want you to break her trust. If that's the case, then I will not pursue this any further. Thank you for coming here."

Gaapa's disappointment was obvious.

"She asked nothing of me," Death said. "Sabnock is where she wants to be. That should be enough answer for everyone...but...I will inform her of your concerns."

"Thank you. That's all I ask," Gaapa replied.

Nodding It's head, Death vanished. Gaapa quickly followed. Wherever It went she wasn't far behind.

* * *

Contrary to the beliefs of many, demons did sleep. In fact, they loved those moments when the unbelievable became real. Gaapa had just finished transporting seventy souls and decided to take a quick nap. What lasted for only a few minutes could feel like hours or days.

"Gaapa," a voice called, interrupting her dream. Gaapa stirred slightly, her eyelids flickering. "Wake up. I need your services." The voice was insistent.

Opening her eyes, Gaapa looked around. Everything in the domov was in order.

Weird dream!

"I'm not a dream, Gaapa. This is Sabnock. I need you to do something for me."

Sitting up, Gaapa rubbed her eyes.

"Sabnock? Is it really you?"

"Yes. I have only a short time and then I must go. Will you help me?"

"Of course, but where are you?"

"Where I should be. I am happy, Gaapa. That's all that matters."

Gaapa nodded. For Sabnock to be happy was almost unimaginable.

"What do you need of me? I'm yours to command."

Sabnock quickly explained what she wanted Gaapa to do.

"I will be eternally grateful," she said when she was finished.

"It isn't your gratitude I want, Sabnock. Just knowing you are well and happy is enough. Thank you for honoring me with this final mission."

"Thank you, Gaapa. Now, I must go. My best to Gaap."

Before Gaapa could reply, she felt the essence of Sabnock vanish.

"Farewell," she said to the emptiness.

* * *

Yemaya and Dakota were snuggled up on the couch in front of the fireplace. Lost in their own thoughts, neither had spoken for almost an hour. Finally, Dakota decided to break the silence.

"I can't help thinking about Constance and Sabnock. What could an historian and a demon have in common?"

"The same thing we have...love," Yemaya said.

"But we're both human. So is Constance...but Sabnock...I mean if she's a demoness...she has to be immortal. It would be an impossible situation."

"Nothing is impossible...and remember, Constance lived a long life. There was plenty of opportunity for them to spend a lot of time together."

"I guess. Still..."

Her next comment was interrupted when the flames in the fireplace began flaring. A loud popping noise followed. Then sparks flew out onto the marbled floor. Both Yemaya and Dakota jumped up and began stomping on the glowing embers scattered near them.

"Green wood," Yemaya said, pushing the charred remnants into a neat pile with her hands. "I will get Maria to bring in–" A scream brought her to her feet. She swung around expecting to find Dakota had burnt herself on an ember. Instead a hideously disfigured woman stood before them holding an object in her hands.

"You are the human, Dakota?" she said, ignoring Yemaya, who had stepped close to Dakota to defend her.

"Ye...Yes," Dakota stammered.

225

"This is yours." Holding it out with her hand, the woman waited for it to be taken. Hesitantly, Dakota took it, her eyes widening in surprise. "I don't understand. Where did you get this?"

"Sabnock asked me to bring it to you. She said you would know what to do with it. Do you?" When Dakota didn't answer immediately, the woman frowned, making her appear more gruesome. "Do you?" she asked again, demanding an answer.

"I...Yes, I know how important it is. We'll protect it," Dakota replied.

The woman looked at Yemaya for confirmation. A slight nod was all she needed to know her mission was over.

"Then I have fulfilled my obligation to Sabnock."

"But..." The question went unanswered. The woman had disappeared. Dakota looked up at Yemaya and then at the manuscript in her hand.

"This is the history of the Gebians."

"I know," Yemaya said.

When Dakota began crying, Yemaya wrapped her arms around her lover and rocked her gently back and forth.

"Do you think they're together?" Dakota asked, sniffling.

"Do you have any doubts now?" Yemaya countered.

"No. No, they have to be together. Constance and Sabnock. I'm happy for them."

"So am I," Yemaya said, squeezing Dakota in a gentle hug.

"I wonder who that woman was. I know this sounds awful but she was so hideous looking." Dakota grimaced.

Yemaya laughed.

"The messenger, I guess. Hopefully, this will be the last time we see that face."

Neither heard the faint laughter coming from the fireplace.

The End

About The Author

FRAN HECKROTTE lives in the Sunny South with her husband, her dogs, fish, chickens and geese. Her life experiences include living in Alaska, gold panning, bull riding, scuba diving, flying, training gaited horses and more. After spending five years in law enforcement, she switched to construction and eventually opened her own property management company. Favorite town is Montréal. Hobbies include gardening, beaches, skiing, photography and reading. Feel free to email her at franheck@hotmail.com.

About the Copy Editor

CINDY BURKE has had a lifelong interest in journalism and fiction writing. She started as a newsroom assistant and has contributed several articles to local newspapers. Her science fiction book, "Intimate Space: A Feminist Utopian Romp Through the Galaxy," was published in 2015.

Burke is a social justice advocate and member of the Clemson Alumni Society for Equality (CASE), an alumni group that supports LGBTQIA initiatives. She can be reached at CindyBurke.com.

Her family is spread across the Southeast, including two sons, a sous chef and a navy technician. Burke lives with her husband, a computer analyst and fellow sci-fi and fantasy buff, in the foothills of the beautiful Blue Ridge Mountains.

About the Cover Artist

PATTY G. HENDERSON is an author, publisher and artist and all around bohemian at heart. An independent author, she launched her own publishing imprint, Blanca Rosa Publishing. She writes Gothic Historical Romances and has published four so far, THE SECRET OF LIGHTHOUSE POINTE, CASTLE OF DARK SHADOWS, PASSION FOR VENGEANCE, and SHADOWS OF THE HEART. She has also penned four Brenda Strange Supernatural Mysteries.

Comfortable wearing several creative hats, Patty is an accomplished artist as well as author. She's done popular book cover artwork for many mainstream mystery and horror authors and lesbian authors via her graphic arts business, Boulevard Photografica, in addition to a nearly complete immersion in indie writing and publishing. You can reach Patty via her author web site: www.pattyghenderson.com or check out her graphics and book cover professional web site: www.boulevardphotografica.yolasite.com.

Other Titles by Fran Heckrotte
The Illusionist (First in the Illusionist Series)

DAKOTA DEVEREAUX, an investigative journalist, is on a mission to uncover the secrets of Yemaya, the Illusionist. However, in her quest for an exposé on this mysterious woman, she uncovers more than she bargained for. Dakota is targeted by a power hungry CEO determined to learn the Illusionist's secrets at all costs, and a madman intent on fulfilling his perverted fantasies.

From Moldova, land of the legendary werewolf, to Transylvania and the Carpathian Mountains, two souls must battle the dark forces of evil for their lives and their love.

* * *

Bloodlust (Second in the Illusionist Series)

YEMAYA AND DAKOTA have just returned to the Illusionist's homeland for a well-earned vacation when they are informed that several villagers have been savagely attacked and killed by something or someone.

At the same time, a young Carpi woman is found lying unconscious near the outskirts of Teraclia. Comatose, she is unable to tell anyone what has happened and science can provide no answers. Two small wounds on her throat raise the old specter of the vampire, a legend the locals of the Transylvanian community are very familiar with and still believe to this day.

The Illusionist and her partner search for the truth behind these attacks. Will they fall prey to the murderous bloodlust that surrounds them, or will they succeed in stopping this heinous reign of terror?

* * *

Lilith (Third in the Illusionist Series)

YEMAYA, the Illusionist, and her journalist partner, Dakota, find themselves embroiled in a search for the person responsible for the rape and torture of a young Carpi woman attending a university in the States. When they decide to visit a local nightclub for "women only," they find the owner and her employees unusual.

Dakota feels mysteriously attracted to one of the clientele while Yemaya recognizes a kindred spirit in Lilith, the club's owner. Spiritual ancestors, missing whores, a sadistic exporter and new acquaintances lead the two lovers into an adventure of Biblical proportions.

Lilith! She was a demoness, as old as humanity itself. Now she is the owner of a "women's only" nightclub and part owner of the Sisterhood, a small group of whores who have banded together to create a better life for themselves. It is her job to protect the women who are putting so much trust in her.

When a local pimp decides to eliminate his competition, Lilith and her two demon partners want revenge and no one knows better how to exact it than demons. This is a revelation of the past, the present and the events that forever changed the course of human history.

* * *

Les Gris, The Shadow People (Fourth in the Illusionist Series)

THEY ARE LES GRIS, the Shadow People, and they are as much a part of us as we are them. As children we talked to them, played with them and disclosed our innermost fears, secrets and dreams, and they patiently listened, comforted and encouraged us.

In time, though, most humans outgrew their *imaginary* friends and eventually forgot them. For those few who didn't, humanity's very existence would be determined by the strength of the bond between a small group of women and their life partners, the *les gris*.

* * *

Saira (Fifth in the Illusionist Series)

SAIRA WAS A TRAVELER. Even her name meant 'traveler'. Her entire existence was dedicated to making the journey to seek answers to the questions that plagued her. Sometimes she felt as if she were a pawn in a game she didn't understand, but she knew her destiny was hers to decide.

She chooses to let the uncertainty of time make the decisions for her. Unfortunately, her curiosity not only gets her into trouble but creates a series of events that affects not only the mortal world but the spirit world too. Yemaya, Dakota, Mari and Maopa will find their lives turned topsy-turvy and Saira will learn an emotion she had never experienced before...fear.

* * *

233

Warrior Demoness (Sixth in the Illusionist Series)

SHE WAS SABNOCK, a demon who, like the Phoenix, lived and died many times because she chose to live amongst mortals rather than spend eternity babysitting the legions of the Underlord. There were no longer battles to be fought in the Underworld, so the ex-commander left her realm to live with the humans as a human.

Falling in love, she now had to choose between her vow to live and die as a mortal or live and love as a demon, not knowing if her lover could accept the truth. The wrong decision would condemn her to a life of loneliness — and for a demon, life was eternity.

* * *

Solaria (Futuristic Science Fiction)

THE FIRST AWARENESS of existence was a chaotic flash of colors, meaningless and yet in an odd way logical, why, she wasn't sure. Birth is the most significant event in life, and yet it is never memorable, at least not for the newborn, but then she really wasn't a newborn, even though it was the first day of her life.

She is 1A526, the first of her kind, an artificially intelligent blend of technology and bio-mechanics. Created to serve humans, Solaria, along with her AI programmer Carley, soon discovers that the company funding the Hubot Project has sinister motives.

For Solaria to fulfill the hopes of the woman who gave her existence meaning, she would have to become the human her programmer dreamed of. She would have to take down Future Dynamicon, the company that created her.

* * *

Future Perfect (Sequel to Solaria)

PRIMERIS WAS a Hubot, designed to serve humans. Her existence depended on her ability to complete her assignments...which she always did with a cold, emotionless detachment.

Now, her perfect record is going to be tested to its limits. In her attempts to find and capture Solaria, another Hubot, Primeris is forced to either disobey her directive of obedience or become the human she never wanted to be.

The Order of the Healers was exactly that, healers. Their mission was to move humanity forward, even if it meant saving the worst of mankind. Chantelle is a Singer, a member of a small sub-group of Healers, whose latest calling takes her on a mission that will test her gift to its limit, and leave her wondering if her success will lead to humanity's downfall.

* * *

Rapture, Sins of the Sinners - Second Place Winner in the 2014 Rainbow Awards
Co-authored with A. C. Henley

A serial killer is targeting young lesbians throughout the state of Texas. Texas Ranger Cochetta Lovejoy thinks she knows who it is and will do everything within her power to stop the person, even if it means stretching the limits of the law.

Detective Agnes Kelly-Elliott is one of Ft. Worth Police Department's finest investigators. When Ranger Lovejoy appears at a crime scene, Agnes fears a dark secret, if revealed, could destroy her family ties and end her career.

This is a dark, gritty, graphic tale of desire gone awry, and flawed characters looking for redemption in all the wrong places.

* * *

Odyssey of the Butterfly

Visit distant worlds. Spend intimate moments with an elderly lesbian couple. Venture into a future when death becomes a living nightmare, and experience a reality where dying is a way of life. Five short stories with a common thread: the butterfly – illusive, mysterious and perhaps even magical. Follow the odyssey. Enjoy the journey.

Back Cover Summary
Warrior Demoness
Book VI in The Illusionist Series

SHE WAS SABNOCK, a demon who, like the Phoenix, lived and died many times because she chose to live amongst mortals rather than spend eternity babysitting the legions of the Underlord. There were no longer battles to be fought in the Underworld, so the ex-commander left her realm to live with the humans as human.

Falling in love, she now had to choose between her vow to live and die as a mortal or live and love as a demon, not knowing if her lover could accept the truth. The wrong decision would condemn her to a life of loneliness — and for a demon, life was eternity.

www.ingramcontent.com/pod-product-compliance
Lightning Source LLC
Chambersburg PA
CBHW051454170626
46811CB00002B/473